RUNNING WILD

RUNNING WILD

A Pictorial Tribute to the NFL's Greatest Runners

By Beau Riffenburgh and David Boss

Designed by Steven Escalante

 A National Football League Book

Prepared by National Football League
Properties, Inc., Creative Services
Division.

First printing, August, 1984

1 2 3 4 5 6 7 8 9

PRINTED IN TOKYO, JAPAN,
BY DAI NIPPON PRINTING CO., LTD.

Contents

THE RECORD HOLDERS

When **Walter Payton** was at Jackson State, he was the greatest scorer in college football history. Before he retires from the NFL, he will be the greatest rusher in pro football history. Payton, like Jim Brown, has rushed for 1,000 yards seven times in nine years. He currently is the number-three rusher on the NFL's all-time list (11,625 yards), but should pass Brown and Franco Harris in 1984. He also should break Brown's record for career 100-yard games (58—Payton now has 54). Payton's biggest game came in the 1977 season (when he led the NFC in rushing for the second of five consecutive years). Against the Vikings, he ran for an NFL single-game record of 275 yards.

It wasn't until my first 200-yard game, against New England in the 1973 season opener, that I was able to say to myself, "I'm as good as anybody in this game."

For me, that was the first time all comparisons to Jim Brown, or at least the reports that put me in his class, seemed valid. Gaining 250 yards against the Patriots was the first time I was totally satisfied with my performance.

Then, I knew going into the last game of the season against the Jets that there was no way they were going to keep me from breaking Brown's single-season record. We knew we were going to win the game. And we knew we were going to get the 61 yards I needed to pass Brown. But I never would have imagined, in my wildest expectations, going over 2,000 yards for the season.

We almost got the 61 yards in the first quarter. When I'd gone past Brown, and after all the hugs and kisses, Reggie McKenzie said, "Now you can relax, Juice. We can go for 2,000."

Late in the game, Joe Ferguson came into the huddle and said, "O.J., you need fifty yards to reach 2,000." I didn't want to hear him say that. It was cold, it was miserable, and the Jets were hittin'.

The play that put me over 2,000 was a power play over Reggie and tackle Dave Foley. I couldn't believe it. I remember thinking then, even though I couldn't articulate it at the time, that this was what I'd be remembered for.

I normally don't set goals. My only goal was to be the best running back I could be. And this was it.

O.J. Simpson

At one time in the NFL, there was no such thing as a running back. Sure, guys set up behind the line of scrimmage, they carried the ball, they got dirty, their teams even ascribed to the "establish the run first" theory. But they weren't called running backs. Football was a different game with different positions.

In the early years of the NFL, most teams used the Single Wing formation, which had been pioneered by Glenn S. (Pop) Warner and brought into pro football by Jim Thorpe of the Canton Bulldogs in 1916. The Single Wing had four backs, the most important of which was the left halfback, or tailback. Early tailbacks such as Sammy Baugh and Dutch Clark called the signals, received most of the snaps from center, ran, passed, and, frequently, kicked. The right halfback, or wingback, in the Single Wing lined up outside the right end and primarily was a blocker, but also ran with the ball, most notably on the inside reverse. The fullback was a burly up-the-mid-

dle runner who also received the snap occasionally, such as on the "spinner" play. Unlike today's quarterback, the Single Wing quarterback was simply a blocking back who considered one carry a game to be heavy-duty work.

Throughout the 1920s and 1930s, NFL teams tried other formations (most simply were variations on the Single Wing theme), but none caught on like the original Single Wing. The Packers used the Notre Dame Box, the Redskins the Double Wing, and the Giants the A Formation. And the Bears, under George Halas and Ralph Jones, made a bold departure from the Single Wing by using the T formation with man-in-motion, which featured fullback Bronko Nagurski and halfback Beattie Feathers. Eventually, defenses caught up; the Lions and Packers solved the mystifying T by rotating their defensive backs to the side of the motion.

After studying the strengths and weaknesses of the T, Clark Shaughnessy, the coach of the University of Chicago (and later of Stanford, Maryland, Pittsburgh, and the Los Angeles Rams), converted it from a moribund formation into a bold, new attack based on quickness and deception. His addition was a counter play, in which he split one end wide, motioned away from him, and ran back to the spread side. In 1940, Shaughnessy guided Stanford to an undefeated season and also found time to design the Chicago Bears' offense that destroyed Washington 73-0 in the NFL Championship Game. The T formation, with its full-house backfield and undeniable strengths, supplanted the Single Wing. The modern running back was soon to follow.

World War II put offensive development in the NFL on hold, but by the late 1940s and early 1950s, several things had combined to give NFL rushing offenses much the same look they have today. First, in 1949, free substitution was permanently adopted in the NFL, allowing full platooning with offensive specialists. Second, the T formation came into general use—the Philadelphia Eagles were the second team to adopt the T (in 1941), and the Pittsburgh Steelers were the last NFL team to drop the Single Wing in favor of the T (in 1952). And third, in 1950, Los Angeles Rams head coach Joe Stydahar and his offensive assistant, Hamp Pool, split halfback Elroy (Crazylegs) Hirsch out as a second wide receiver, leading the way toward what became the accepted NFL standard of having two wide receivers and two backs behind the quarterback.

Even then, however, backfield development was not totally complete. Through the 1950s and most of the 1960s, the NFL officially divided the split backs behind the quarterback into different positions—halfback and fullback. Fullbacks generally were bruising power runners, such as the Browns' Marion Motley and the Bills' Cookie Gilchrist. Halfbacks were supposed to have the speed to get outside (which most did) and the fluid, deceptive moves of Hugh McElhenny or Gale Sayers (which only McElhenny and Sayers really had) without the fullback's size. That distinction slowly died as Vince Lombardi's Green Bay Packers won championship upon championship in the 1960s with two fullback-sized backs—Jim Taylor (nominally the fullback) and Paul Hornung (listed as a halfback). At about the same time, San Francisco had the ultimate set of big backs in Ken Willard and John David Crow, although the 49ers didn't win a league title until 1981. Going the other way, the Dallas Cowboys lined up tough little fullback Don Perkins next to halfback Dan Reeves, who actually was the bigger of the two. Making the trend on the field official, in 1967 the NFL adopted the generic term "running back."

Almost as soon as backs were designated runners, however, they took on

Jim Brown was the ultimate running back, possessing both power and speed. Even after his career records are broken, his feats really won't have been equaled. He led the league in rushing eight times in his nine-year career. When he retired in 1965, he held 20 NFL records, including yards rushing in a career (12,312), season (1,863), and game (237). He also held career records for carries, average yards per carry, 100-yard games, 200-yard games, 1,000-yard seasons, rushing touchdowns, and total touchdowns. Perhaps his most impressive statistic was that, despite repeatedly setting the record for carries in a season, he still holds an NFL career record with a 5.22-yard average per carry.

*If **Gale Sayers** wasn't perhaps the greatest outside threat in NFL history, he would be remembered as the greatest kick returner. As a rookie in 1965, the "Kansas Comet" was second in the NFL in rushing, punt returns, and kickoff returns, and led the league with a record 22 touchdowns (14 rushing, 6 receiving, and 1 each on punt and kick returns). That year he also tied the all-time record by scoring six touchdowns in a game against the 49ers. Sayers led the league in rushing in 1966 and 1969, and might have led it in 1967 and 1968 if he hadn't been injured midway through each season. He also led the NFL in kickoff returns in 1966 and remains the leading kickoff returner in NFL history (30.56-yard average).*

another function. In the mid-1970s, Lydell Mitchell of Baltimore and Chuck Foreman of Minnesota led the way as running backs began to lead the league in receiving. That trend reached a high point in 1983, when a running back was the number-one or number-two receiver for 11 of the 14 NFC teams.

In the last two years, a significant change has been made in the look of NFL running attacks. Reflecting the continued emphasis on the passing game, many teams have started using two tight ends and one lone running back. The Washington Redskins currently even use both a one-back fullback in John Riggins, and a one-back halfback in Joe Washington (himself a former league receiving leader), alternating them depending upon the situation.

Running Wild is a tribute to all of these runners—to the big backs and little backs, to the fullbacks and halfbacks, to the backs who lined up in a full-house, in a split backfield, or by themselves. It is a pictorial history that begins in the late 1940s when the position began to resemble its modern version. It was then that players, specializing on offense or defense, truly became what we know as "running backs" and not two-way tailbacks, wingbacks, or, simply, "backs."

The following pages are a celebration of the running back and of his personal on-the-field signature. Running backs are individuals. The function and style of Earl Campbell, Tony Dorsett, and Marcus Allen are almost as diverse as those of Bill Dudley in the Single Wing and Eric Dickerson in the one-back formation. Similarly, Jim Brown, Franco Harris, and Walter Payton, the three running backs recently crowding the NFL rushing throne room once occupied by Brown alone, are as distinct as can be. Brown was the perfect fullback, thundering up the middle, stomping would-be tacklers into the dirt. Harris is the gliding runner who starts and stops, side-stepping those who try to bring him down. And Payton is the quick, slashing runner with the power to be an inside runner, the quickness to dart outside, the temperament to block like a lineman, and the versatility to catch, throw, and return kicks.

"Who actually can compare running backs?" asks Red Grange, the Hall of Fame back who almost single-handedly popularized pro football in the 1920s. "I don't know what it is that makes one back run better than another. It's not just speed, because some of the worst football players I've ever seen were track stars. I'd say a runner needs to have a number of qualities, including great balance, a sense of timing, quickness, strength, good field vision, and a natural instinct. And to be a great runner, you need more, you need something special."

Those players with that something special—something that allowed them to become the record holders in the NFL—are the focus of Chapter One. There are only nine of them—Jim Brown, Earl Campbell, Eric Dickerson, Tony Dorsett, Franco Harris, Walter Payton, John Riggins, Gale Sayers, and O. J. Simpson—but they are the men whose names dot the *NFL Record and Fact Book*. They can be found among the career leaders, in the records section, and among the 1,000-yard rushers, where their names seem to pop up again and again. If, despite the words of Red Grange, you can pick the greatest running backs in NFL history, they are on the pages that follow.

O.J. Simpson *might be the best running back in the history of college football. He was just as effective in his 11-year NFL career. The Heisman Trophy winner from USC took a couple of years to get untracked in the NFL, but then he turned in five 1,000-yard seasons in a row, including four (1972-73, 1975-76) in which he led the league in rushing. In 1973, he set the NFL record for yards rushing in a season (2,003) and a game (250), the latter a record he broke in 1976 (273 yards). He retired as the number-two rusher in NFL history with 11,236 yards.*

In 1983, **Franco Harris** gained 1,007 yards to close in on a record many once thought impossible to break: Jim Brown's career rushing mark. That season, Harris also became the NFL's number-two career rusher (11,950 yards). Harris also is the record holder for most carries in a career (2,881) and most 1,000-yard seasons (8). Despite his success in the regular season, Harris has saved many of his best days for the playoffs. He holds almost every important playoff career rushing mark, including carries (394), yards (1,523), and touchdowns (17).

A number of people thought Heisman Trophy winner **Tony Dorsett** was too small to play in the NFL when the Dallas Cowboys drafted him in 1977. But Dorsett changed that thinking in a hurry. He not only ran for more than 1,000 yards as a rookie, he did it in each of his first five years in the NFL, extending his 1,000-yards-per-season streak to 11 years, including 2 years in high school and all 4 at the University of Pittsburgh (where he became college football's all-time rusher with 6,082 yards). Although Dorsett's streak was snapped in the strike-shortened 1982 season, he set another record when, against the Minnesota Vikings on national television, he ran 99 yards for a touchdown. In 1983, he started a new 1,000-yard string (1,321) as he ran his career total to 8,336 yards.

In his first year in the league, the Rams' **Eric Dickerson** got his name in the NFL record book four times. Not only did he set NFL rookie records for carries (390), yards rushing (1,808), and touchdowns rushing (18), his carries were an all-time high for any runner. The number-two pick in the 1983 college draft out of SMU, Dickerson twice gained more than 190 yards in a game as a rookie.

For sheer power up the middle, few backs ever could compare with **John Riggins.** One of only three backs to rush for more than 1,000 yards with two different teams (the Jets and the Redskins), the man nicknamed "The Diesel" has become the number-five rusher in NFL history with 9,436 yards. He was named the most valuable player in Super Bowl XVII after gaining a then-game record 166 yards. The following season, 1983, he set NFL records by rushing for 24 touchdowns and scoring touchdowns in 13 consecutive games.

Few backs ever exploded onto the NFL scene like Houston's **Earl Campbell** in 1978. The Heisman Trophy winner from Texas led the NFL in rushing with a then-rookie record 1,450 yards. The next year he increased his league-leading total to 1,697 yards, and in 1980 he led the NFL with 1,934 yards, the second-most ever. He also set four NFL records in 1980, including most 100-yard games in a season (11), and in a row (7). Campbell led the AFC in rushing in 1981 and was second in 1983. After just six years he has moved into the number-nine all-time spot on the career rushing chart (8,296 yards), with the best per-season average (1,382.7) in NFL history.

WHEN MEN WERE MEN AND 1,000 YARDS WAS 1,000 YARDS

In 1934, Beattie Feathers of the Chicago Bears became the first back in professional football history to rush for 1,000 yards in a season. The mark then was considered almost a fluke. No one else at that time had gained much more than 800 yards in a season, and it appeared that Feathers's 1,004 yards (on only 101 carries) would remain a record forever.

It did last a long time—until 1947, when a powerful halfback named Steve Van Buren led the Philadelphia Eagles to their first title ever while gaining 1,008 yards. Van Buren did as much as anyone to assure the continuing popularity among coaches of the T formation, of power football, and of the off-tackle run. And his accomplishments helped make 1,000 yards a realistic goal for the better runners in the league. Slowly— ever so slowly—that goal began to be reached. In 1949, Van Buren did it again, rushing for 1,146 yards. That same year, Tony Canadeo of Green Bay became the league's third 1,000-yard rusher (1,052). But through the next nine years, only San Francisco's Joe Perry (1,018 in 1953 and 1,049 in 1954) and Chicago Bears fullback Rick Casares (1,126 in 1956) joined the new club.

Throughout the 1950s, and even in the 1960s, when the NFL expanded its schedule from 12 to 14 games, 1,000 yards was more than a legitimate goal for the league's superstars. By 1969, the fiftieth anniversary of the NFL, only 22 backs had gained 1,000 yards in a season, and of them only 3—Jim Brown, Jim Taylor, and Leroy Kelly—had done it more than twice. Some of pro football's Hall of Fame greats, such as Hugh McElhenny, Ollie Matson, Lenny Moore, and Charley Trippi, never made it.

Brown and his successor at Cleveland, Kelly, were responsible for one of the most amazing streaks in NFL history. From 1958 through 1968, only once did one of them not rush for more than 1,000 yards. In that time, Brown first broke Van Buren's record by almost 400 yards (gaining 1,527 in 1958), and then shattered his own mark by more than 300, when he piled up 1,863 yards in 1963. He finished with seven 1,000-yard seasons in nine years. Kelly, who gained more than 1,000 yards each of his first three years as a starter, remains, along with John Henry Johnson, the most outstanding eligible running back not in the Pro Football Hall of Fame. The only year in that string the Browns didn't have a 1,000-yard rusher was 1962, when, coincidentally, a then-record six backs did reach the mark: Taylor, Johnson, and "The Scooter," little Dick Bass of Los Angeles, in the NFL; and, in the young American Football League, Cookie Gilchrist of Buffalo, Abner Haynes of the Dallas Texans, and Charlie Tolar of Houston, who became the first three backs in AFL history to surpass 1,000 yards. Only once again (1967) would three backs gain that many yards in one season in the 10-year history of the AFL.

In the 1970s, the 1000-yard club began to lose its exclusivity as teams began to spread ball-carrying duties around less and less. The NFL went from a time when four or five players on a team would have a substantial number of carries to the extensive use of only two and (more recently) one back per team. In 1956, for example, the San Francisco 49ers' backfield depth included McElhenny, Perry, J.D. Smith (another 1,000-yard man), and Johnson (who twice would rush for 1,000 yards with the Steelers). The four of them carried the ball a total of 10 times *less* that year than Los Angeles Rams rookie Eric Dickerson did in 1983 alone.

The 1,000-yard barrier began to crumble most noticeably in 1978, when the NFL went to a 16-game schedule, requiring only 62.5 yards per game to reach 1,000 in a season. The credibility of 1,000 yards as a measure of greatness reached a low point in 1983, when a record 16 backs gained more than 1,000 yards. The standard still denoted excellence, but greatness may be another story. By comparison, it had taken more than 30 years, from 1932 (when the NFL first started keeping official statistics) to 1966, for 16 backs to gain 1,000 yards in a season.

Most of the marks established by the running backs who gained more than 1,000 yards before 1970 have since been eclipsed. But they haven't been surpassed in quality. Yards—today frequently equivalent to carries—don't tell the whole story. When Green Bay's Jim Taylor ran for more than 1,000 yards five consecutive seasons (1960-64), only once did he average less than 4.8 yards per carry. When Franco Harris broke Taylor's record with six 1,000-yard seasons in a row (1974-79), he never averaged *more* than 4.8 yards per carry.

The backs pictured in this chapter are 17 of those 22 who gained more than 1,000 yards before 1970 (not including Feathers, Brown, Jim Nance, Gale Sayers, and Paul Robinson, who are featured elsewhere). They belong to a select group—those who gained 1,000 yards the hard way.

*If there was anything **Steve Van Buren** couldn't do, NFL defenders never knew about it. He was a big, powerful sprinter with the determination of a blocking back, which he was at LSU. Van Buren led the NFL in punt returns as a rookie in 1944. The next year he led the league in rushing (the first of four times), scoring, and kickoff returns. He twice set the NFL single-season rushing record—in 1947 with 1,008 yards, and two years later with 1,146. In the Eagles' 14-0 victory in the 1949 NFL Championship Game, he set records with 31 carries and 196 yards.*

*Versatile **Tony Canadeo** was Green Bay's leading passer before he went into military service in 1945. When he rejoined the Packers, the "Silver Fox" (as he was known for his premature white hair) became their power runner, enjoying his best year in 1949, when he became the third NFL back to gain 1,000 yards in a season (1,052). The 5-foot 11-inch Canadeo played 11 years with the Packers.*

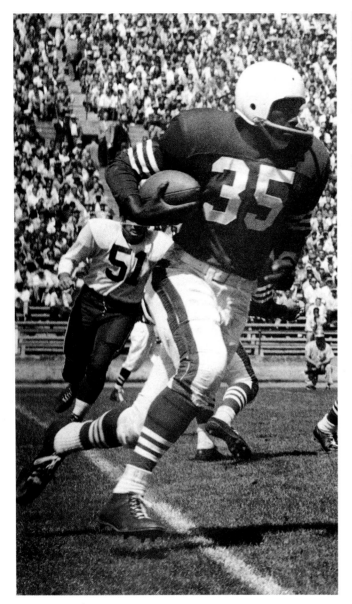

Unquestionably the greatest eligible player not yet in the Pro Football Hall of Fame, **John Henry Johnson** played 13 years with four teams. His first three years were spent as a member of San Francisco's "Million Dollar Backfield." Then, in 1957, he led Detroit in rushing, and combined with Bobby Layne and Tobin Rote to lead the Lions to the NFL championship. But Johnson's best statistical years came after he was traded to Pittsburgh (1960-65). There he was reunited with Layne and twice (1962 and 1964) rushed for more than 1,000 yards.

In the NFL, 1956 was the year of **Rick Casares.** The powerful fullback led the league in carries (234), yards (1,126), and touchdowns (12). He also led the Bears to the best record in the NFL (9-2-1) and to the NFL Championship Game, where he scored Chicago's only touchdown.

In **Joe Perry's** rookie season (1948) with San Francisco, he led the AAFC in yards per carry. Five years later, he became the fourth NFL back to gain 1,000 yards in a season, and the next year the first to do it in consecutive seasons. Five more years into his career, he led the NFL in yards per carry. And five more years afterward, he returned from a two-season stint in Baltimore to finish his career with the 49ers. Perry's career lasted an amazing 16 years —a record for running backs. In that time, he ran for 9,723 yards (including his two seasons in the AAFC).

Paul Lowe didn't waste any time earning a reputation. On the first play of his pro career—the first play in Chargers history—he returned a kickoff 105 yards for a touchdown. Lowe went on to be an all-AFL choice four times, including 1965, when he set the league record of 1,121 yards rushing and also was voted AFL player of the year. He was named to the all-time AFL team.

Abner Haynes was one of the first stars of the AFL. He signed with the Dallas Texans in 1960 after a college career at nearby North Texas State. In 1960, he led the AFL in rushing (with 875 yards) and punt returns, and the Texans in receiving and kickoff returns. Two years later, Haynes helped take the Texans, who became the Kansas City Chiefs in 1963, to the AFL championship with 1,049 yards. He still ranks as Kansas City's number-two all-time rusher.

J.D. Smith had to get his start in the NFL as a defensive back, because of some other San Francisco backs named John Henry Johnson, Joe Perry, and Hugh McElhenny. But in his third year, Smith was moved to offense, where he proceeded to lead the team in rushing five consecutive years. His best year was 1959, when he gained 1,036 yards, second in the NFL only to Jim Brown.

In 1954, an 18-year-old giant (6-3, 246) known as *Cookie Gilchrist* signed with the Cleveland Browns right out of high school. Although he didn't make the team, Gilchrist was determined to play pro football. He went to Canada, where he was an all-league fullback (and all-league problem, playing for four different teams despite his ability). In 1962, Gilchrist signed with the Buffalo Bills and became the first AFL player to gain 1,000 yards (1,096) in a season, while also gaining a reputation for his vicious blocking. He again led the league in rushing in 1964. As he had in Canada, Cookie ran to a different drummer—for three different AFL teams.

Dick Bass was not exactly a household name when the Rams drafted him in the first round in 1960. Despite leading the nation in rushing, total offense, and scoring as a junior, Bass hadn't been given much credibility because he played at the College of the Pacific. After a 10-year career in which he became the Rams' all-time leading rusher, Bass (at 5-10, 200, known as "The Scooter") finally had received the recognition he deserved. He twice gained more than 1,000 yards (1962 and 1966) and played in three Pro Bowls.

Charlie Tolar spent much of his career being the "other guy" in the Houston backfield alongside Billy Cannon. But Tolar, the AFL's original "human bowling ball" (at 5 feet 6 inches, 200 pounds), was quite productive on his own. In 1962, he rushed for 1,012 yards on an AFL-record 244 carries.

Look up the word "tough" in a dictionary, and you'll see a picture of **John David Crow.** The 1957 Heisman Trophy winner at Texas A&M (where he played for Bear Bryant), Crow (6-2, 222) was the heart of the Cardinals' offense in the late 1950s and early 1960s. His best year statistically was 1960, when he ran for 1,071 yards. In 1965, he was traded to San Francisco, where he was teamed with Ken Willard in one of the best (and biggest) backfields ever.

When Jim Brown retired after the 1965 season, the Browns' offense was supposed to collapse. But it didn't—**Leroy Kelly** took over and the Browns didn't miss a beat. They made the playoffs more often behind Kelly than with Brown. Kelly hadn't gotten much notice his first two years despite leading the NFL in punt returns in 1965. But in 1966, he finished second in the NFL in rushing (1,141 yards), and then finished first each of the next two years (1,205 yards in 1967 and 1,239 in 1968). Kelly ended his career as the number-four rusher in NFL history (7,274 yards).

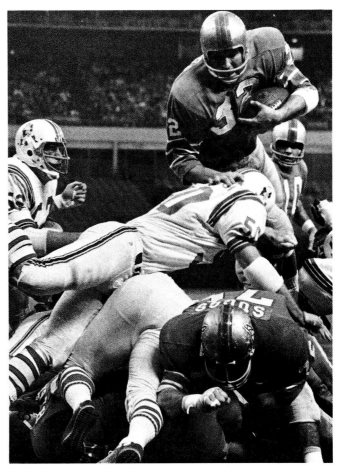

Clem Daniels carried the ball only one time for minus two yards as a rookie with the Dallas Texans in 1960. The next year, however, he joined the Oakland Raiders and went on to become the leading rusher in the history of the AFL with 5,101 career yards. Daniels led the Raiders in rushing six consecutive years; in 1963 he set the AFL season mark with 1,099 yards.

More often than not, **Hoyle Granger** was the entire offense for the Houston Oilers through the late 1960s. Big (6-1, 225), strong (with enormously powerful legs), and tough, Granger was the number-two rusher in the AFL in 1967 (1,194 yards), when the Oilers won the Eastern Division title. He had another productive season to lead them to the playoffs in 1968. But as injuries limited his effectiveness, the Oilers lost their place among the title contenders.

Mike Garrett holds a unique place in NFL history: He was the first player ever to rush for more than 1,000 yards with different teams. Garrett (5-9, 195), who had won the Heisman Trophy at USC and then helped the Chiefs to Super Bowl I as a rookie, exploded in his second year (1967) for 1,087 yards. In Super Bowl IV, he scored the game's first touchdown. He again reached the 1,000-yard mark in 1972, gaining 1,031 with the Chargers. He finished his career among the top dozen NFL rushers of all time.

THE POWER BROKERS

*More powerful than a locomotive (and some defenders would swear bigger than one, as well), **Marion Motley** broke defenses for eight years with the Cleveland Browns. Motley was the career rushing leader in the AAFC with 3,024 yards. He led the league in 1948 (964 yards), and never finished lower than fourth in the season rushing statistics. Motley led the NFL in rushing in his first season, 1950 (810 yards).*

"This comment may surprise most people, coming from me," Red Grange once said, "but, to be honest, it's the guys who power up the middle, the guys who will lay down that all-important block for you, the guys who will take the ball, stick their heads into a linebacker, and make that fourth-and-short a first-and-ten, who win football games."

In the NFL, the quarterbacks, the big-play wide receivers, and the break-away halfbacks usually seem to get the headlines. But it is the fullbacks who traditionally have been the first concern of the defense. Their punishing drives behind the center or off tackle have made championship teams go. Even when Grange still was playing with the Bears, he wasn't the real threat. He had to take a back seat to his fullback, Bronko Nagurski. When the Bears won the first official NFL Championship Game in 1933 (23-21 against the New York Giants), it was Nagurski who ran for a game-high 65 yards and *threw* two touchdown passes. Nagurski also had led the team in rushing during the regular season with 533 yards, compared to 277 by Grange.

Nagurski was but one of a herd of fullbacks who thundered through the NFL in the 1930s and 1940s. Jim Musick of the Boston Redskins, Hall of Famer Tuffy Leemans and powerful Bill Paschal of the Giants, and Clarence (Pug) Manders of the Brooklyn Dodgers all led the league in rushing despite rarely running to the outside. The modus operandi of each was the same, best expressed as, "I'm coming through the middle. Why don't you just see if you can stop me?"

One could say that fullback as a position began to mature in 1946 (as did the NFL itself in many senses). With the offensive genius of one man, Paul Brown of the Cleveland Browns, and the athletic ability of another, Marion Motley, fullback expanded into a versatile, multi-purpose position, while maintaining its traditional focus on power up the middle. Watching Motley was much like viewing an enormous oak tree on a rampage. He had the girth of any two other backs and the speed to run past any defensive halfback who imagined he could hold onto Motley's bulk. In his first four years, Motley became the old All-America Football Conference's all-time leading rusher, while helping the Browns to four consecutive championships. The perfect complement to Otto Graham's passing, Motley popularized the draw and trap plays and helped establish the fullback as a receiver.

Although Motley led the NFL in rushing in 1950, the year the Browns left the defunct AAFC to join the older league, he did not long remain the dominant fullback in pro football. The team the Browns defeated in the 1950 championship game, the Los Angeles Rams, had two youngsters—Deacon Dan Towler and Paul (Tank) Younger— who soon would join in one backfield with another fullback (Dick Hoerner) to form one of the largest and most unstoppable combinations in history, the "Bull Elephant" backfield. In 1951, Towler, Younger, and Hoerner each averaged more than six yards per carry, a feat that only one other running back in the entire NFL achieved. Another fullback, Eddie Price of the New York Giants, led the league in rushing. The following year, Towler was the NFL's top rusher.

For the next two decades, NFL teams kept trying to find another Marion Motley. A number of big fullbacks came and went through pro football, the most successful of whom was Jim Taylor of Green Bay. Taylor ran for more than 1,000 yards five consecutive seasons, led the league in rushing in 1962, and was the main offensive force in four of Green Bay's championship years. The most successful of the other big fullbacks have been Alex Webster (the all-time leading rusher for the Giants), Jim Nance (who set the AFL single-season rushing record of 1,458 yards in 1966 with the Patriots), Ken Willard (the number-two career rusher with the 49ers), and, most recently, Pete Johnson, the Bengals' career rushing leader, who now plays for the Chargers.

At the same time Motley and the Bull Elephants seemed to be convincing the football world that a fullback's size and power were directly related to his success, another man quietly started out to prove otherwise. Joe Perry was a short, squat speedster nicknamed "The Jet" for his explosive starts. He played pro football for 16 years, finishing his career as the number-two rusher in NFL history and leading the league in rushing in 1953-54. Despite his statistics, playing on teams with Hugh McElhenny, John Henry Johnson, Y. A. Tittle, and John Brodie limited Perry's national visibility. But to the players in the NFL, he was one of the most feared runners, most feared blockers, and most feared men among tacklers in the league—and for good cause.

In 1950, Perry was blind-sided by George Connor of Chicago and suffered two broken ribs. Two years later, Perry broke loose on a trap up the middle in a game against the Bears. Running in the open field, with only Connor between him and the end zone, Perry didn't fake. He built up a head of steam, lowered his helmet, and barreled into Connor, dropping him on the spot. Although Perry, slowed by the collision, was caught a few steps farther on, the debt had been paid.

Toward the end of his career, Perry spawned a host of "Joe Perry-type" backs. Bill Brown of Minnesota and Don Perkins of the Dallas Cowboys were the best of the small fullbacks, although neither had the speed of Perry. Perkins's successor in Dallas was perhaps the toughest, most determined of the bunch. Walt Garrison was known to play when he hardly could walk. But he would get taped from his shoulders to his feet, and then take his mummy act to the field, where he was as unstoppable as his Egyptian counterpart. And he was the picture of consistency.

"If you ever need four yards," Dallas quarterback Don Meredith once quipped, "Walt Garrison will get you four yards. If you need eight yards, Walt Garrison will get you four yards."

If you had wanted those eight yards, the best fullback to go to would have been Jim Brown. During nine years with the Browns (1957-1965), he set virtually every NFL rushing record of consequence. And he did end one argument: Did NFL teams want a big, powerful fullback or a little, quick fullback? Neither, it turned out. They all wanted Jim Brown. But the attempts to find another Brown failed. Curtis McClinton was big and quick for the Chiefs, Earl Gros had all the makings of a superstar if he had started for a championship team instead of the hapless Philadelphia Eagles and Pittsburgh Steelers, and Cookie Gilchrist and Wray Carlton were bruisers for Buffalo. But none of them was Jim Brown—by a long shot.

A charter member of the Rams' "Bull Elephant" backfield, **Paul (Tank) Younger** officially spent a lot of time at halfback, but, like Los Angeles running mates Dan Towler and Dick Hoerner, he really was a fullback. The big (6-3, 230) Grambling product was the first player drafted from an all-black school (in 1949) and was the first of many great Grambling players in the NFL. He played his final year in the same Pittsburgh backfield as Tom (The Bomb) Tracy.

Of all NFL fullbacks, Larry Csonka came closest to achieving Brown's kind of dominance of the position. Ironically, the great Syracuse coach Ben Schwartzwalder (who also coached Brown), desperately wanted Csonka to play guard. Once moved to fullback, however, Csonka was unstoppable, both in college and the NFL. He was the essence of Miami's undefeated team of 1972, opening the way for Mercury Morris's outside thrusts and Bob Griese's pinpoint passing with his crushing runs behind guards Larry Little and Bob Kuechenberg.

"I wouldn't have ever wanted to be a halfback," Csonka once said. "I like running up the gut. You see, a power runner can intimidate the defense. And if not, at least you can nail them once in a while. Linebackers spend their entire careers beating up on ballcarriers who are twenty or thirty pounds lighter than they are. So I love to run in the middle and even the score a little for the offense."

Deacon Dan Towler might have become a minister after he retired from the NFL, but he sure gave opposing defenses hell for six years (1950-55) with the Rams. Towler, who had exceptional speed for his size, led the NFL in rushing in 1952, when he averaged 5.8 yards per carry running almost entirely up the middle. He finished his career as the leading rusher in Rams history (3,493 yards).

Pat Harder helped lead the old Chicago Cardinals to the most successful season in the franchise's history. As a second-year player in 1947, Harder joined halfbacks Charley Trippi and Marshall Goldberg and quarterback Paul Christman to form the original "Million Dollar Backfield." That year the Cardinals won the NFL championship and Harder won the first of three consecutive scoring titles, during which time he became the first NFL player to score more than 100 points in three different seasons.

For a full decade (from the mid-1950s to the mid-1960s) it really was **Alex Webster** *who made the New York Giants go. Webster's bruising inside runs occupied defenses and opened up the outside for an offense that also featured Y. A. Tittle, Frank Gifford, and Del Shofner. Two decades after he retired, Webster still remains the Giants' leading career rusher with 4,638 yards.*

Curtis McClinton *still is remembered by old-time AFL defenders as one man to avoid. He had a reputation as an all-world runner at Kansas, and added to that with his crushing blocks during eight years with the Chiefs (1962-69). McClinton lined up first next to Abner Haynes, and then Mike Garrett, but he wasn't just a blocker. He still ranks as Kansas City's number-four career rusher (3,124 yards).*

Wray Carlton *didn't always line up at fullback—since Buffalo also had Cookie Gilchrist—but he always ran and blocked like one, no matter how they listed him. Carlton led the Bills in rushing their first season and, by the time he retired, had become the franchise's all-time leading rusher with 3,368 yards. The 235-pound Carlton was teamed with Bobby Burnett and Keith Lincoln late in his career, but was most effective when he and the 246-pound Gilchrist just could grind defenses down.*

Perhaps no other back in NFL history has combined durability with consistency like **Bill Brown.** Brown played 14 years in the NFL, 13 with Minnesota. If the Vikings needed three yards, the man with the flat-top haircut would get it, no questions asked. Brown was as versatile as he was tough— when he retired, he held Minnesota career records for rushing (5,757 yards), receptions (284), and touchdowns (76), and he still was serving as captain of the special teams. He also was the blocker that helped make reputations for Tommy Mason, Dave Osborn, and Chuck Foreman.

Jerry Hill was never a household name like Johnny Unitas, Lenny Moore, and Tom Matte, with whom he lined up. But, without Hill, those other Baltimore back-field stars might not have been, either. Hill succeeded Alan Ameche as the Colts' fullback in 1961. For the next decade, he provided the Colts their inside threat, pounding out enough yards (2,668) to retire as the number-four rusher in Baltimore history.

Quick, who was the fullback at Syracuse before Larry Csonka? The answer is **Jim Nance** (one of a series of great Syracuse runners—Jim Brown, Ernie Davis, Nance, Floyd Little, and Csonka) But the man who set the all-time AFL single-season rushing rec-ord doesn't need trivia questions to be remembered. Nance joined the Boston Patriots in 1965 and led them in rushing the next six years. His second year he set the AFL rushing mark with 1,458 yards, and the next season again led the AFL with the second most yards in league history (1,216).

The Dallas Cowboys thought so highly of **Don Perkins** that Clint Murchison signed the University of New Mexico star to a personal services contract before the franchise had officially been granted. Perkins lived up to those expectations—he wasn't flashy, but he was incredibly consistent. In eight years, he led the Cowboys in rushing seven times, played in six Pro Bowls, and never gained less than 614 (or more than 945) yards. He finished his career in 1968 as the number-five rusher in NFL history with 6,217 yards.

Hewritt Dixon *started his career with the Denver Broncos as a tight end. Four years later, however, he was obtained by Oakland and moved to fullback, where the Raiders took full advantage of his versatility. In 1967, he finished fourth in the AFL in receiving (59 for 563 yards) and eighth in rushing (559 yards). The next year, he was third in rushing (865 yards) and thirteenth in receiving (38 catches for 360 yards). He retired as Oakland's number-two career rusher (2,960 yards) and number-three career receiver (190 receptions).*

One of the most durable "big men" of all time, **Ken Willard** *missed only one game in his first eight years in the NFL. During that time, he led San Francisco in rushing seven times, gained 5,930 career yards, and teamed with John Brodie to lead the 49ers to their first three division titles ever (in 1970, 1971, and 1972). He spent his last season with coach Don Coryell and the St. Louis Cardinals, whom he helped lead to the playoffs for the first time in 26 years.*

In 1970, when the Raiders and Chiefs were vying for the AFC West title, **Marv Hubbard** was Oakland's secret weapon. Hubbard had played little as a rookie in 1969. He didn't see much more action in 1970—except in the two games against Kansas City, when he ran for 98 and 93 yards (of a season total 246) to help earn Oakland the title. The next four years were different. He led the Raiders in rushing four consecutive times (including a team-record 1,100 yards in 1972) and finished as the club's number-two career rusher with 4,399 yards.

Walt Garrison just might be the toughest running back, pound for pound (6-0, 205), in NFL history. The man who used to be called "The Cowboys' Cowboy" had been an Oklahoma State Cowboy as well as a rodeo star. In 1969, called upon to replace Don Perkins, he gained 818 yards and helped block Calvin Hill to rookie of the year honors. Although nagged by injuries, Garrison still played, and played hard, for nine years. He would look like he could hardly walk, would wear up to 25 yards of tape, and then would drag half the defense three extra yards for a first down.

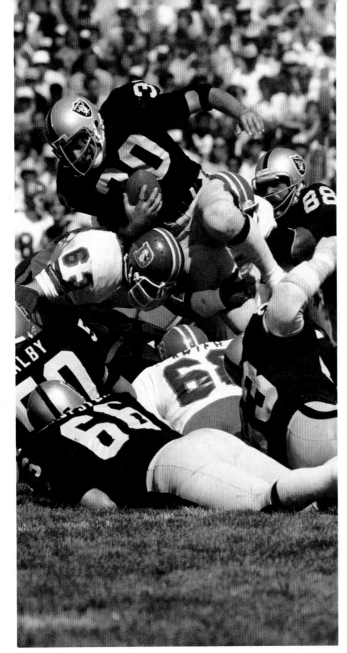

It took Colgate's powerful **Mark van Eeghen** to replace Colgate's powerful Marv Hubbard as the fullback for the Oakland Raiders. Van Eeghen earned a starting position as a second-year player and went on to appear in an amazing (for a running back) 107 consecutive games. He gained more than 1,000 yards three straight seasons and led the AFC in rushing in 1977 with 1,273 yards. Before finishing his career with the Patriots, he became the leading rusher in Raiders history and number-14 all-time in the NFL (6,650 yards).

Jim Otis was an All-America at Ohio State, but it took him four years in the NFL with three teams before he finally found himself as a pro. In 1974 Otis pounded out 664 yards with St. Louis. The next year he kept on the roll, and gained an NFC-leading 1,076 yards. He retired after 1978 as the Cardinals' all-time leading rusher with 3,863 yards.

Sam Cunningham was an unusual first-round draft choice—a USC fullback. He wasted no time establishing his pro credentials, leading New England in rushing as a rookie. He also led the Patriots in rushing five other years (including 1,015 yards in 1977), and finished his career as the number-one rusher (5,453 yards) and number-three scorer (49 touchdowns) in club history.

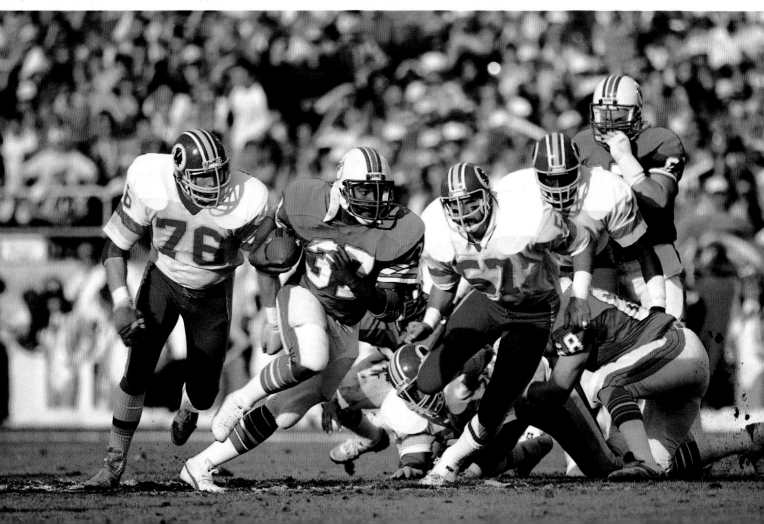

< **George Rogers** won the Heisman Trophy at South Carolina in 1980, but the next year he was even better. In his first season with the New Orleans Saints, Rogers set a rookie rushing record of 1,674 yards on an NFL-record 378 carries. Entering the 1984 season, he was only 34 yards short (3,353 yards) of becoming the leading rusher in Saints history.

The big fullback reached its logical extreme in **Pete Johnson,** who weighed in somewhere between 250 and 280 pounds. Johnson, who played in the same backfield with two-time Heisman Trophy winner Archie Griffin, finished his Ohio State career as the number-four touchdown scorer in NCAA history with 53. He then led the Cincinnati Bengals in rushing each of his seven years with the team, and became the club's career rushing and touchdown leader with 5,421 yards and 70 touchdowns. He was traded to the San Diego Chargers before the 1984 season.

< **Andra Franklin** spent his career at Nebraska blocking for I-backs Rick Berns, I.M. Hipp, and Jarvis Redwine. But when he joined the Dolphins, the husky (5-10, 225) Franklin became the star. In 1981, he set Miami rookie rushing records. The next year, he was third in the NFL in rushing (701 yards) and was named to the AFC-NFC Pro Bowl. In 1983, he led the Dolphins in rushing for the third consecutive time.

THE HANDYMEN

In 1967, the term "running back" was conceived to describe the function of the two backs lined up behind the quarterback, and to distinguish them from the fourth back, the flanker (who, two years later, also received a new name—wide receiver). For a long time there had been backs who did little else besides carry the ball, and there still are some. But there always have been, and always will be, backs who do much more than that. Officially they're running backs, but they also are receivers, passers, blockers, kick returners, and, usually, exceptional winners.

Multi-purpose backs flourished in the pre-World War II days, when most everyone played both ways and many teams ran the Single Wing. And that pattern still was prevalent several years after the war, as teams became accustomed to free substitution. Bill Dudley, for example, led the NFL in rushing, interceptions, and punt returns in 1946, while also leading the Pittsburgh Steelers in passing, scoring, punting, and kickoff returns.

The first of the modern T formation all-purpose backs, however, was Charley Trippi, a Single Wing tailback at Georgia who, while with the Chicago Cardinals, was primarily a halfback for five years, a quarterback for two, and a defensive back for two. Another back who could do it all, who helped the Lions into three NFL championship games, who won two NFL scoring titles, and who should one day be voted into the Pro Football Hall of Fame, was Detroit's Doak Walker. Walker joined with quarterback Bobby Layne, halfback Bob Hoernschemeyer, and fullback Pat Harder in one of the best, and most diverse, backfields in NFL history.

When the platoon system became common, all-purpose backs began to simply return kicks and catch passes, as well as run. The 1950s and early 1960s were dominated by such players. The zig-zagging, cross-field runs of Hugh McElhenny, the extra "kick" of Olympian Ollie Matson, the hard cuts and fingertip catches of Lenny Moore, the intellectual and athletic grace of Frank Gifford, and the "solid on the field, flashy off" approach of Paul Hornung all went toward one end—moving the football into the end zone in more ways, with more styles, than ever before.

The next generation of handymen didn't receive quite the fanfare of those celebrated 1950s multi-purpose backs, with one exception—Gale Sayers. In 1966, Sayers led the league in rushing and kickoff returns and was third among full-time running backs in receiving yards. He finished his career as the NFL's all-time leading kick returner (30.56-yard average), finished second in yards per carry (5.00), and (although he didn't have enough returns to qualify) averaged almost two yards (14.5) per punt return more than the career record.

The closest 1960s running back to Sayers in versatility (and one who lasted longer) was Philadelphia's Timmy Brown, who once was described as "Ollie Matson Junior." A twenty-seventh-round draft choice by Green Bay in 1959, Brown was an early Vince Lombardi cut who went on to gain more than 12,000 all-purpose yards and score 64 touchdowns. He even returned a missed field goal a record 99 yards for a score.

An even more productive back was Bobby Mitchell. For four years the versatile halfback lined up next to Jim Brown. Then he was traded to Washington in 1962 for the rights to Heisman Trophy winner Ernie Davis of Syracuse. The Redskins moved Mitchell to flanker, where he led the NFL in receiving yards two consecutive years and averaged more than 30 yards per kickoff return. He occasionally played halfback again before retiring in 1968, at which time he ranked third in career receiving (521 catches), second in all-purpose yards (14,078), fifth in career touchdowns (91), and tenth in kickoff return average (26.4 yards).

During the late 1960s, running backs were considered versatile if they simply could catch the ball. In those days, 30 or so receptions were enough to rank a running back among the league's top backfield receivers. The best of the rusher-receiver backs were Tommy Mason of Minnesota and Los Angeles (who also was an outstanding kick returner until knee injuries eliminated his special teams participation), Joe Morrison (who was so effective for the Giants that he never knew if he would line up as a halfback or flanker until game day), former tight end Hewritt Dixon of the Raiders, Tom Woodeshick of Philadelphia, and big Ken Willard and John David Crow of San Francisco.

A couple of backs added a new dimension, which actually wasn't new at all. Dan Reeves of Dallas and Tom Matte of Baltimore, two former college quarterbacks, were feared throughout the league for their halfback passes. Reeves's successor, Calvin Hill, continued the tradition for Dallas.

The early 1970s fostered a new breed in the NFL. When teams saw Kansas City win Super Bowl IV behind Hank Stram's three mini-backs—Mike Garrett, Robert Holmes, and Warren McVea, who each were 5 feet 9 inches—short backs became the order of the day. And the little, versatile, but tough back became a fixture in the league. In 1974, 5-foot, 5-inch Mack Herron (the shortest NFL player since 5-foot 4-inch Buddy Young tore up the league in the early 1950s) broke Sayers's NFL record for all-purpose yards with 2,444. The next year, 5-foot 10-inch Terry Metcalf broke that with 2,462 yards. But neither Herron nor Metcalf had the longevity of Greg Pruitt of the Los Angeles Raiders, who, in his eleventh year in 1983 (and after three 1,000-yard rushing seasons with Cleveland), set the NFL record for punt return yards in a season. The most up-to-date version of the mini-back, James Brooks, now plays in Cincinnati after three record-breaking seasons in San Diego.

The mid-1970s again redefined the meaning of "all-purpose." Impressed by the results of two backs who led their conferences in receiving in 1975—Baltimore's Lydell Mitchell and Minnesota's Chuck Foreman—coaches began to design more of their passing attacks around throwing short, safe passes to backs. The result was that for eight consecutive years at least one conference was led in receiving by a running back. Baltimore alone had running backs who led the AFC in receiving four times—Mitchell in 1974, 1975, and 1977, and Joe Washington in 1979.

As the NFL entered the 1980s, it no longer was just an advantage to have running backs who could make receptions. It was a necessity. If a back couldn't catch, the

If there ever were a catalyst for a team's rise to the top, it was **Charley Trippi.** *He joined the Chicago Cardinals in 1947, and that year the Cardinals won the Western Division title, after finishing fourth in 1946. In the NFL Championship Game victory over the Eagles (28-21), Trippi ran 44 yards on a frozen turf for one touchdown and returned a punt 75 yards for another. Trippi could do everything on a football field well, and his 5.1-yard career rushing average is still the fourth best in NFL history. Due to unique wartime rules, Trippi (a Single Wing tailback at Georgia) played in four Chicago College All-Star Games as a collegian. He was elected to the Pro Football Hall of Fame in 1968.*

There seemed to be no way that **Doak Walker,** *who won the Heisman Trophy as a junior at SMU, could live up to his billings in the NFL. But the man who many consider to be the finest overall back in the history of college football did. As a rookie he led the NFL in scoring with 128 points, the second most in NFL history at the time. He led the league again in 1955 with 96 points. Walker helped take the Lions to three NFL championship games, and scored the deciding points in both of the victories (1952 and 1953). He retired after only six years having more than doubled the old Lions' record for career points scored (with 534).*

only way he'd get on the field was with the crowd tearing down the goalposts after the game. Pass receiving no longer was listed under the "versatility" category.

Certain backs, though, still do a lot of other things for their teams. San Diego's Chuck Muncie, the Los Angeles Raiders' Marcus Allen, and Chicago's Walter Payton all help keep defenses off-balance with halfback passes. Payton has shown he can return kicks, too; he led the NFL in kickoff returns as a rookie. Pruitt, Brooks, Stump Mitchell of St. Louis, and Darrin Nelson of Minnesota (the NFC's leading kickoff returner in 1983) all contribute on return teams as well. Joe Washington is perhaps the best example of a multi-purpose back who thrives on situational substitution. He generally comes in on long-yardage downs, when his receiving skills and skittering, elusive, breakaway dashes are most dangerous.

No matter how these backs are used, they all form part of the modern contingent that seems to be going about trying to prove that there's much more involved in being a running back than running.

Grace, style, and class all described Hall of Famer **Frank Gifford,** but (more important to the New York Giants) so did production. After beginning his career concentrating on defense, Gifford became one of the best run-catch combination men in NFL history. In 1956, he led the Giants to the NFL championship. That year he gained 819 yards and caught 51 passes, marking the first time in history a back had been in the top five in the league in both categories. Gifford missed all of 1961 after being injured in 1960, but returned as a flanker in 1962 and averaged more than 20 yards per catch. For his career, he ran for 3,609 yards, caught 367 passes (then a Giants' record) for 5,434 yards, and scored 78 touchdowns.

>

<

Little (5-4, 170) **Buddy Young** was one of the most exciting players in the history of pro football. Young joined the New York Yankees of the All-America Football Conference in 1947, where he teamed with the fabulous Spec Sanders. As a rookie, Young was third in the Eastern Conference in rushing (712 yards and a 6.1-yard average), third in receiving (27 receptions), second in kickoff returns (27.0-yard average), and second in punt returns (15.9-yard average). After the AAFC folded, Young played with the New York Yanks, Dallas Texans, and Baltimore Colts in the NFL.

You name it, **Dick James** did it. The little (5-9, 170) scatback from Oregon was one of the last NFL players to play both ways in games with any regularity. He was in the NFL 10 years, 8 with Washington. The first time he touched the ball for the Redskins, he ran 83 yards with the opening kickoff of the 1956 preseason. Two years later, he was chosen the offensive and defensive player of the game against the Eagles. For his career, James totaled 1,930 yards rushing, 1,629 receiving, and 5,639 on returns. He also intercepted 10 passes and led the NFL in punt returns in 1963.

>

The Los Angeles Rams so coveted **Ollie Matson** that they traded nine players to get him in 1959. Matson was big (6-2, 220) and fast; he won a bronze medal in the 1952 Olympics in the 400-meter run. He also was incredibly productive. In his 14-year career, he ran for 5,173 yards, caught passes for 3,285 more, returned kicks for 3,746 yards (a 26.2-yard average), and scored 73 touchdowns. He was inducted into the Hall of Fame in 1972, his first year of eligibility.

The only problem with **Lenny Moore** was that the Colts couldn't give him the ball on every play. That was fortunate for the rest of the NFL—Moore was as dangerous as anyone in the league, both as a runner and as a receiver. Three times he averaged more than seven yards per carry, and twice he averaged more than 20 yards per catch. The sleek (6-1, 198) Hall of Famer from Penn State scored 113 career touchdowns, the second most in NFL history, ran for 5,174 yards, and caught passes for 6,039. His best year was 1958, when he gained 598 yards rushing—a 7.3-yard average—and caught 50 passes for 938 yards.

New York Giants' opponents must have thought **Joe Morrison** would play forever. He just about did. In his 14-year Giants career, Morrison was a running back and a wide receiver—sometimes both in the same game. He also played defense and once even worked out at quarterback. In 1969, his eleventh season in the NFL, he led the club in rushing, receiving, and scoring. Currently, Morrison is the head coach at South Carolina. He still is the leading receiver in Giants history with 395 receptions for 4,993 yards.

Bobby Mitchell started his career as one of the top running backs in the NFL; he ended it as one of the top receivers. For four years at Cleveland, Mitchell was the halfback next to Jim Brown. During that time he averaged 5.4 yards per carry, caught 128 passes, and scored 38 touchdowns. In 1962 he was traded to Washington, where he led the league in receiving. The next year, he caught a 99-yard touchdown pass and led the league in receiving yardage. During his first six years in Washington, Mitchell never caught fewer than 58 passes. When he retired in 1968 he was the number-two receiver in NFL history with 521 receptions. He was named to the Hall of Fame in 1983.

Perhaps the major reason the Minnesota Vikings were so effective early in the club's history was the play of **Tommy Mason.** In 1963 Mason ran for 763 yards, caught 40 passes, and averaged 15.8 yards on punt returns. Mason was traded to Los Angeles midway through his career; his versatility helped the Rams dominate the Coastal Division under head coach George Allen in the late 1960s.

Dan Reeves ranks as one of the great free-agent finds ever. A record-setting quarterback at South Carolina, he signed with the Dallas Cowboys in 1965. The next year he ran for 757 yards, caught 41 passes, scored 16 touchdowns, and terrorized NFL secondaries with his halfback passes. Although he injured a knee in 1968 and never regained his starting position, he was a valuable reserve in the Cowboys' first two Super Bowl appearances. Today he is the head coach of the Denver Broncos.

Timmy Brown's first year as a pro was spent on the bench with Vince Lombardi's Green Bay Packers, which is understandable considering that he was a twenty-seventh-round draft pick. In 1960 Brown signed as a free agent with the Eagles (the Packers had cut him) and his career took off. He played on the Eagles' 1960 championship team and retired after helping Baltimore win the 1968 championship. In between, he established himself as one of the most versatile backs in the NFL. He ran for 3,862 yards, caught passes for 3,399 more, returned kicks 4,781 yards (a 26.0-yard average), and scored 64 touchdowns. In 1965, he was third in the league in rushing (861 yards) and tenth in receiving (50 catches).

Eugene (Mercury) Morris was "Mr. Outside" to Larry Csonka's "Mr. Inside" on Miami's Super Bowl winners. Morris twice finished second in the nation in rushing (behind O.J. Simpson) at West Texas State. With the Miami Dolphins he initially was an out- standing kick returner and scat- back. But in 1972, when Miami went 17-0, he was a starter and gained 1,000 yards. The next year he rushed for 954 yards and a league-leading 6.4-yard average.

Mack Herron only played three years in the NFL, but the 5-foot 5-inch, 170-pounder left his mark. In 1974, he set the NFL record for all-purpose yards (2,444), rush- ing for 824, catching 38 passes for 474 more, returning punts for 517 (a 14.8-yard average), and returning kicks for 629. He led the Patriots in all four categories.

No one could believe it when the Dallas Cowboys used their first draft choice of 1969 on **Calvin Hill** of Yale. But as a rookie, the big (6-4, 227) Ivy Leaguer fin- ished second in the NFL in rush- ing (942 yards) and earned a reputation as the new king of the halfback pass. Hill twice gained more than 1,000 yards, including the 1972 season, when he ran for 1,036, made 43 receptions, and threw a 55-yard touchdown pass. He also played with Washington, and finished his career with Cleveland as a third-down back. For his career, he gained 6,083 yards and caught 271 passes.

A record-setting Wishbone half-back at Oklahoma (where he averaged 9.4 yards per carry as a junior), **Greg Pruitt** initially was thought to be too small to play in the NFL. Twelve years later, he still is around. Pruitt has gone through the entire cycle of being a running back: He started as one of the league's top kick and punt returners, was installed as Cleveland's heavy-duty ball carrier (gaining more than 1,000 yards three seasons in a row), became a third-down receiving back, and, in 1983 with the Raiders, set the NFL single-season record for punt return yards.

If **Terry Metcalf** had been bigger than 5 feet 10 inches, 180 pounds, he would have been frightening. In five years with the Cardinals (1973-77), Metcalf ran for 3,438 yards, caught 197 passes, and returned kicks and punts for almost 4,000 yards. In 1974, he led the league in kickoff returns, and the next year set an NFL record with 2,462 all-purpose yards. After playing three years in Canada, he joined the Washington Redskins in 1981 for his final season.

Lydell Mitchell is the only man to make Franco Harris and Bert Jones each take a back seat in offensive production. As a senior at Penn State in 1971, Mitchell was an All-America and scored an NCAA-record 29 touchdowns while playing in the same back-field as Harris. With Baltimore in the mid-1970s, he overshadowed Jones, running for more than 1,000 yards three consecutive seasons (1975-77), and catching more than 60 passes four years in a row. In 1974, 1975, and 1977 he led the AFC in receiving.

Rickey Young was mainly a blocking back for Walter Payton in college (at Jackson State), but he made a reputation of his own in the NFL. After three years with San Diego, he joined the Minnesota Vikings in 1978: that year he led the NFL in receiving with 88 catches. In his nine years in the NFL, Young has gained almost as many yards receiving (3,283) as he has on the ground (3,666).

> Perhaps no other big (6-3, 228) back has had the versatility of **Chuck Muncie.** An All-America at California, Muncie was the first draft choice of New Orleans in 1976. He led the Saints in rushing three times and became their career rushing leader, but was traded in 1980 to San Diego. With the Chargers, he has been the perfect complement to Dan Fouts, rushing for more than 3,000 yards, catching almost 150 passes, and establishing himself as one of the best in the NFL at the halfback pass.

< The mid-1970s belonged to O.J. Simpson in the AFC, and **Chuck Foreman** in the NFC. Foreman burst onto the NFL scene in a big way in 1973, earning rookie of the year honors. Two years later he led the NFC in scoring (132 points) and receiving (73 catches); he also gained 1,070 yards rushing. From 1973-78, he rushed for 5,664 yards, caught 317 passes, scored 73 touch-downs, and led the Vikings into the playoffs six consecutive years.

When **Joe Washington** was at Oklahoma (where he gained a then-Big Eight record 3,995 yards), Texas coach Darrell Royal described the little (5-10, 175) All-America Wishbone halfback as "elusive as smoke through a keyhole." Washington's natural abilities have continued to serve him well in the NFL. He was the primary back for three years with the Colts, including the 1979 season, when he ran for 884 yards and led the NFL with 82 receptions. The past three years, he has been an important cog in Washington's offense, leading the team in rushing and receiving in 1981 and finishing second in both categories in 1983.

It is almost impossible to pick out **James Brooks's** strongest area as a running back. He does everything so well. In three years with the Chargers (before he was traded to Cincinnati in 1984), he rolled up some impressive numbers: 1,471 yards rushing, 84 receptions, 587 yards on punt returns, and 2,283 yards on kick returns. Brooks is Auburn's career rushing leader with 3,523 yards. He played in the same backfield as William Andrews and Joe Cribbs.

HEART AND SOUL

"Earl Campbell," said then Houston Oilers' coach Bum Phillips in 1978, "is the kind of player you can build an offense and an entire team around. He is such a dominating runner that he makes linemen look better than they are, the quarterback look better than he is, and, because he allows the offense to control the tempo of the game, the defense look better than it is. And I'm hopin' he'll make me look better than I am."

Campbell helped the Oilers look better, all right. From an 8-6 also-ran record in 1977 (while Campbell was winning the Heisman Trophy at Texas), the Oilers followed their powerful fullback to three consecutive seasons in the playoffs and two appearances in the AFC Championship Game.

Having a player who can dominate a game like Phillips described—and like Campbell proceeded to do—is rare in the NFL, however. Pro football is not like pro basketball or baseball, where a center such as Kareem Abdul-Jabbar or a pitcher such as Nolan Ryan can control the ebb and flow of a game. A talented running back or quarterback can't totally dictate what his own team does, much less what the opposition will do.

Even having a player who can dominate his own offense has been more rare than one might think. It was easy for the Single Wing tailback (such as Dutch Clark, Sammy Baugh, or Bill Dudley) to control the offense, when he did most of the running, passing, kicking, and, significantly, play-calling. But since the modernizations of the World War II era, the quarterback has called the plays and passed, while the running backs have been the center of the ground game. And NFL offenses traditionally have been based on the running attack, thereby keeping a delicate, but definite, balance between the quarterback and running backs.

Occasionally, one player's abilities have dictated his team's offensive philosophy. His importance has been exaggerated by the inability of his teammates in other offensive areas. For example, Sonny Jurgensen may have been the best pure passer ever, but his numbers and importance were increased because the Redskins' running game relied on A.D. Whitfield, Steve Thurlow, Gerry Allen, and Ray McDonald.

Generally, however, for a later T formation team to build itself totally around one player required someone remarkable, a player who could outshine even quality teammates. It also required a remarkable coach, who was willing to use his star to the diminution, or even the exclusion, of any other offensive threats.

Jim Brown certainly wasn't the only star on the Browns. Quarterback Milt Plum led the NFL in passing twice while Brown was on the team, halfback Bobby Mitchell since has been voted into the Hall of Fame, and Gary Collins was one of the league's better receivers. But there is no doubt that Brown was the main man on the team. His running set up Plum's passing, and the number of his carries, while not seeming exhorbitant today, were inconceivable in the early 1960s.

Other 1960-vintage backs didn't have some of the built-in advantages Brown received in Cleveland. Rather, they were helped by the "Jurgensen test" in establishing their importance to the team. As great as Gale Sayers was, there wasn't much of anyone else on the Bears' offense in the late 1960s. Ditto Dick Hoak of the Steelers, Floyd Little of the Broncos, and Tom Woodeshick of the Eagles, three outstanding backs who played for perpetual losers.

Most players' roles have not been shaped simply by measurable abilities, but by their coaches' philosophies. No one has shown that better than some of the dominant running backs of recent years. When head coach Lou Saban rejoined Buffalo in 1972, O. J. Simpson had had three average seasons in pro football. Following Saban's decision to build the Bills' offense around Simpson, O. J. ran for more than 1,000 yards each of the next five seasons, leading the NFL four of those years.

Other coaches have followed the same pattern, including, most notably, Phillips and Chuck Knox. Phillips built the Oilers' offense around Campbell. Then, when he became head coach in New Orleans, he drafted another big fullback in the Campbell mold, George Rogers. Knox, on the other hand, has picked out a back with each of the three NFL teams he has coached and has centered the attack around him, regardless of the quality of his quarterback (and John Hadl, James Harris, Pat Haden, Joe Ferguson, Jim Zorn, and Dave Krieg all are quality quarterbacks). In Los Angeles, Knox made taxi-squad player Lawrence McCutcheon the Rams' all-time rusher; in Buffalo, multi-talented Joe Cribbs was his man; and in Seattle, Curt Warner has a bright future with Knox, who knows how to use him, and will use him . . . and use him . . . and use him. And that is what being a team's main man is all about.

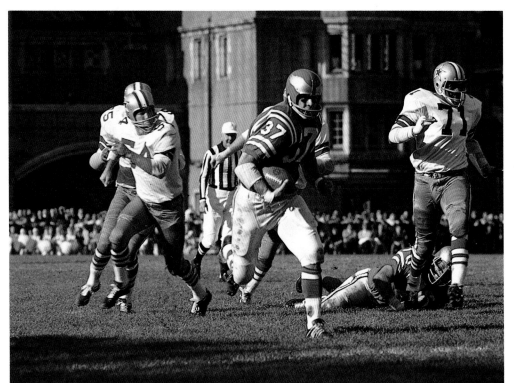

*In 1958, **Jim Brown** ran for a record 1,527 yards; that year the NFL's number-two rusher (Alan Ameche) had 791 yards. The next season Brown shattered the NFL record with 290 carries. In 1960, Cleveland's journeyman quarterback, Milt Plum, led the NFL in passing. Those statistics all are related—when Cleveland came to town, teams concentrated on stopping Brown, leaving the rest of the Cleveland attack to work quietly and efficiently. The biggest problem for a defense, however, was not having the other Browns be more efficient, but not stopping Brown anyway.*

***Gale Sayers** suffered nagging injuries that affected five of his seven NFL seasons. But Sayers finished among the top five NFL rushers five times and led the league twice (1966 and 1969). His efficiency was just as impressive, his average being among the top four in the league four times. Sayers's career achievements (4,956 yards, a 5.0-yard average, and 56 touchdowns) are even more remarkable because he spent much of his career coupled with Jack Concannon, a quarterback who didn't generate a passing game dangerous enough to take the heat off Sayers and the Bears' running game.*

***Tom Woodeshick** is one of the NFL's greatest forgotten men. Philadelphia's eighth-round draft choice in 1963, the compact (6-0, 225) Woodeshick's running style defined "bruising." From 1967 through 1969, Woodeshick's power (gained from his long-term weight lifting) was the only consistent part of the Eagles' attack. He bulled for a career-best 947 yards in 1968 and played in the 1969 Pro Bowl.*

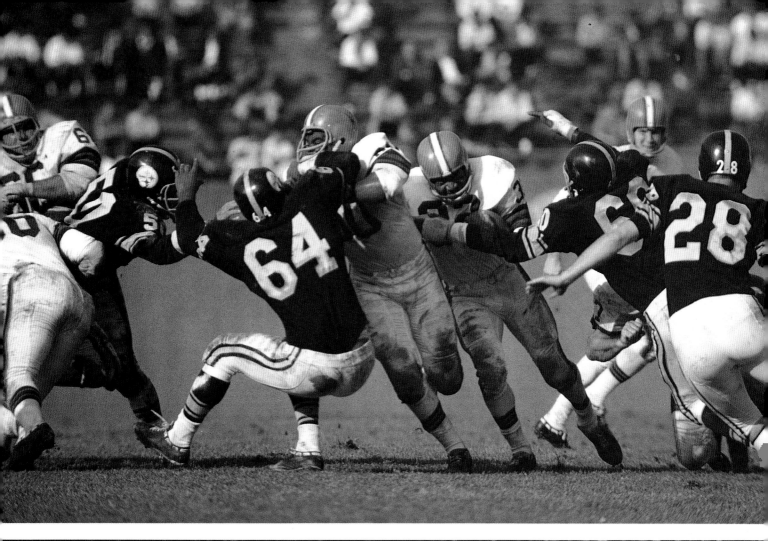

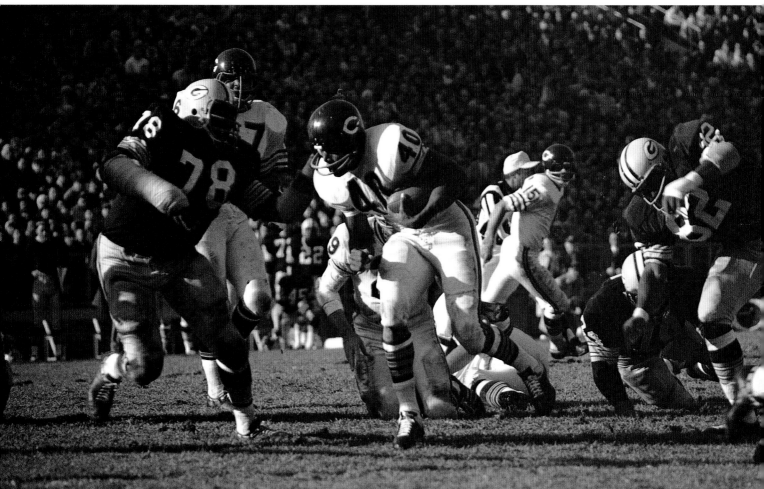

When **Dick Hoak** broke into the Pittsburgh lineup, the other running back was John Henry Johnson. After Johnson left, Hoak had to carry the Steelers' ground attack, with help from a passing game generated by Kent Nix, Ron Smith, Bill Nelsen, and Dick Shiner. Though not overly large (5-11, 190) and virtually on his own in the backfield, Hoak gained almost 4,000 yards to finish his career as the number-two rusher in Steelers history. His best season was in 1968, when he gained 858 yards for an outstanding 4.9-yard average.

Perhaps no running back ever > has meant more to his team than **Larry Brown** did to the Redskins in the early 1970s. An eighth-round draft choice from Kansas State in 1969 (part of Vince Lombardi's only draft with the Redskins), Brown ran for 5,037 yards, caught 159 passes, and scored 50 touchdowns in his first five years. During that period he recorded five of the seven best rushing seasons in Washington history. He was the leading rusher in the NFC in 1970 and again in 1972, when he carried the Redskins to Super Bowl VII. But Brown was small (5-11, 195) for a workhorse role — his production dropped as time wore on and he wore down. He was perhaps the classic case of overuse in NFL history.

<

Floyd Little played nine years for the Broncos when they never had a record better than 7-5-2. Despite not having much backup support, Little twice led the AFC in rushing (1970 and 1971) and finished his career with 6,323 yards, the seventh most in NFL history at the time. Little was a three-time All-America at Syracuse, where he lined up one year with Jim Nance and two with Larry Csonka. He also was an outstanding return man, averaging 11 yards on punt returns and more than 25 on kickoff returns. He played in five AFL All-Star Games or AFC-NFC Pro Bowls.

The man they called "Clutch" spent his first year in the NFL on the Rams' taxi squad. Chuck Knox became the Rams' head coach in 1972, and **Lawrence McCutcheon** was off the bench and into the record book. In his first real season, McCutcheon set a Los Angeles record with 1,099 yards rushing. He ran for more than 1,000 yards three of the next four seasons, breaking his own team record each time in the process. McCutcheon, who played in the Pro Bowl five consecutive years, left the Rams as the club's career rushing leader with 6,186 yards. Perhaps his finest moment, however, came in Super Bowl XIV, when he threw a 24-yard touchdown pass.

Mike Pruitt only may be the number-three rusher in Browns' history, but ranking behind Jim Brown and Leroy Kelly isn't bad—neither is a career total of 6,034 yards. The bull-like (6-0, 225) Pruitt succeeded Greg Pruitt as Cleveland's main ball carrier in 1979, and then proceeded to rush for more than 1,000 yards in four of the next five seasons. He also is an important part of the Browns' passing game; he has 250 career receptions.

With the recent emphasis on the aerial game, virtually every team in the NFL has set club passing records in the past five years. The Chicago Bears, on the other hand, have had only 2 of the team's best 15 passing seasons in the past 20 years. That reflects the emphasis and workload the team has placed on the shoulders of **Walter Payton** in the past nine years. Payton should become the NFL's all-time rushing leader in 1984. Payton's production is matched only by his endurance. He has played in 126 consecutive contests and has missed only 1 game in his career. In that time, he rushed for 11,625 yards, caught 328 passes, averaged 31.7 yards on kickoff returns, threw five touchdown passes, and even averaged 39 yards on punts.

Wilbert Montgomery scored a college-record 37 touchdowns as a freshman and a total of 76 in his career at Abilene Christian. Yet he was available when Philadelphia chose him in the sixth round of the 1977 draft, making him one of the great sleepers in NFL history. Since joining the Eagles, Montgomery has been their driving force. He has had three 1,000-yard seasons (includ-ing a team- record 1,512 in 1979) and helped lead the club to four consecutive playoff appearances. But his lack of size (5-10, 195) has contributed to a series of injuries; without him healthy, the Eagles haven't achieved a winning season. In 1984, Montgomery should pass Steve Van Buren to become the club's career rushing leader.

It took **Earl Campbell** two years and two games to pass Hoyle Granger as the Oilers' all-time rushing leader. Now he ranks ninth on the NFL career rushing list with 8,296 yards. In each of his first three seasons, Campbell was voted the NFL's most valuable player by the Pro Football Writers of America. That gave him the unusual honor of having been named the nation's top high school, top college, and top pro player during his career. In 1980, Campbell was the only player in the NFL to rush for 200 yards in a game. He did it four times, including twice in a row, both NFL records.

Billy Sims left Oklahoma with a Heisman Trophy and career totals that included 3,813 rushing yards, a 7.1-yard average, and 50 touchdowns. He has been just as effective in the NFL. In four seasons, Sims has gained 4,419 yards, led the Lions in rushing each year, and made 155 recep-tions. He returned from a broken hand suffered early in the 1983 season and gained more than 800 yards in the second half of the season. His output was the main force propelling Detroit to its first division title in more than two decades.

James Wilder hasn't gotten much recognition from NFL fans, but it isn't because of his lack of ability. For the first three years of his NFL career, Wilder has been the only consistent feature of Tampa Bay's attack. Wilder joined the Buccaneers after finishing as Missouri's career rushing leader. He started as a rookie, but really blossomed in 1982, when he led the Bucca- neers in rushing (324 yards) and finished third in the NFL in receiving (53 receptions). Despite missing six games in 1983 due to injury, Wilder still led the team in rushing (640 yards, including a club single-game record 219 against Minnesota) and receiving (57 receptions). He currently is the number-three rusher and number-two receiver in Tampa Bay history.

Joe Cribbs was Chuck Knox's main man in Buffalo much as Lawrence McCutcheon had been in Los Angeles. Cribbs wasn't big (5-11, 190), but was extremely durable and versatile. He led the Bills in rushing four consecutive seasons, totaling 4,046 yards. He was Buffalo's leading receiver in 1983 and caught 162 passes in his four-year career. Cribbs was picked in the second round of the 1980 draft with the last choice Buffalo had received from San Francisco in the trade for O.J. Simpson.

When **William Andrews** was at Auburn, he was a Wishbone fullback who spent much of his time blocking for teammates James Brooks and Joe Cribbs. Since entering the NFL, however, he has been one of the most productive backs in league history. In five years, Andrews has gained more than 1,000 yards four times (in- cluding a team-record 1,567 in 1983), and has become the Falcons' career rushing leader with 5,772 yards. He also has caught 271 passes, including a team-record 81 in 1981. In 1983, he became only the second NFL back to gain more than 2,000 yards rushing and receiving in more than one season.

No one who knew pro football had any doubt that **Eric Dickerson** would be a star after his record-setting career at SMU. Dickerson broke Earl Campbell's Southwest Conference career rushing mark (4,450 yards), tied Doak Walker's school record with 48 touchdowns, and finished third in the balloting for the Heisman Trophy. In the NFL, he not only led the league in rushing as a rookie (1,808 yards), he also caught 51 passes and scored 20 touchdowns, the second most in the NFL.

Curt Warner was taken third in > the 1983 NFL draft, one place behind Eric Dickerson. And the former Penn State All-America (who rushed for a school-record 3,398 yards) proved to be just as valuable. Warner became Chuck Knox's third outstanding back (after Lawrence McCutcheon and Joe Cribbs), and is potentially the best. He led the AFC in rushing with 1,449 yards, caught 42 passes, and scored 14 touchdowns (the most in the conference). He was named the AFC's most valuable player and rookie of the year.

Ernie Green had the unusual distinction of playing in the shadow of not one but two great running backs. In his second year out of Louisville (1963) he succeeded Bobby Mitchell as Jim Brown's running mate. He finished with the second-highest average per carry (6.0 yards) in the NFL, trailing only Brown. When Brown retired, Green became even more effective in the backfield with Leroy Kelly. In 1966, Kelly finished second in the league in rushing. Green was seventh (750 yards) and ranked third among running backs with 45 receptions. The next year, he ran for 710 yards, ninth most in the NFL. Green retired after seven years with 3,204 yards and 195 receptions to his credit.

THE OTHER GUY

"Wayne Morris is the hardest working guy on this team," St. Louis Cardinals center and co-captain Dan Dierdorf said in 1982. "He's the hardest practicing guy on the team. He lifts more weights, he watches more film, and he runs farther and harder than anyone else. He works people right into the ground."

The rest of the Cardinals agreed with Dierdorf; in 1982, Morris was voted the team's most valuable player. But to most fans around the NFL, Morris remained "Wayne Who?"

As widely viewed as professional football is and has been, anonymity is one thing still guaranteed to a large number of quality running backs in the league. By the very nature of the game's offensive design and regardless of their contributions to the team, some backs are going to get a lot of acclaim, such as Morris's teammate Ottis Anderson, and some are going to be virtually ignored.

Occasionally there are backfields where more than one rusher gets his share of credit. But that often means that the third or fourth back receives less. The great Army team of 1945, for example, featured two players who would win the Heisman Trophy—halfback Glenn Davis and fullback Doc Blanchard. Even the quarterback, Arnold Tucker, received some All-America mention. But the other back, Tom (Shorty) McWilliams, almost was overlooked completely. It wasn't until McWilliams transferred to Mississippi State after World War II that he received the credit he deserved.

NFL history is dotted with potentially great players who, because they are blockers or because they just don't carry the ball as much as their backfield team-mates, are nearly anonymous when they are playing, and totally forgotten soon afterwards. One can almost assume that, in the NFL, for every star running back there was a forgotten one who helped to make him what he was. To paraphrase the saying, "Behind every great runner, there is a blocking back."

One of the first "other guys" was Bosh Pritchard, who teamed in the same back-field with Steve Van Buren. On most any other team, Pritchard would have been a star, but with the Eagles he lived in the long shadow of Van Buren. In 1949, Pritchard led the NFL in yards per carry while finishing ninth in the league in rushing—but Van Buren was the all-pro after leading the NFL in rushing.

When he was in Cleveland, Bobby Mitchell was one of the best kept secrets in pro football. He did everything for the team, including flash enough talent to challenge Jim Brown, and push him to work even harder to maintain his premier status. But the rushing yards (2,297 in four years), receptions (521 in his career), return yards (27.0-yard kickoff return average and 10.3-yard punt return average), and blocking that eventually got Mitchell to the Hall of Fame weren't enough in those golden days.

To the public, he was just another fellow catching the Jim Brown Express.

Even gaining the traditional standard of 1,000 yards hasn't been enough to assure star status. In 1972, when Miami went 17-0, Mercury Morris gained 1,000 yards, but teammate Larry Csonka gained 1,117 and the headlines. Four years later, Rocky Bleier of Pittsburgh rushed for 1,036 yards and a 4.7-yard average. But teammate Franco Harris got the acclaim. Despite averaging only 3.9 yards, Harris gained a little more (1,128). Besides, it was his fourth 1,000-yard season, so everybody knew him.

Sometimes, the lesser known backs' main function—or sole responsibility—is to block. The epitome of the blocking back, the back who is content to rarely carry the ball and to help the main man in the backfield go, was Tim Wilson of Houston. Wilson was a big (6-3, 230), solid power runner from Maryland who looked to be a talented NFL running back, until the Oilers drafted Earl Campbell. As Campbell's importance—and carries—increased, Wilson's carries went down. He ran the ball 126 times (to Campbell's 302) in 1978. Each of the next three years he saw the ball less frequently, until, in 1981, he had but 13 attempts for 35 yards.

The NFL is full of underpublicized backs today. The best probably plays, believe it or not, in a one-back formation. Joe Washington of the Washington Redskins is the man *when* he's in the game. The Redskins have built their offense around big, powerful John Riggins, who carried the ball 375 times in 1983 (the third most in NFL history). Washington plays either on long-yardage situations or, occasionally, when Riggins needs a rest. Despite his lack of playing time in 1983, Washington gained 772 yards (enough to lead nine other teams in rushing yardage), for an NFC-high 5.3-yard average. He also caught 47 passes. That's not the same kind of opportunity Riggins had. Then again, it's pretty good for the "other guy."

For five years in the mid-1970s > **Jim Bertelsen** *of the Rams was the best-blocking running back in the NFL. The man who made Lawrence McCutcheon go wasn't a bad runner, either, as his 853 yards in 1973 and selection to the 1974 Pro Bowl indicate. One reason for Bertelsen's comparative blocking ability was that he was the first Wishbone halfback in the NFL. (He had been at Texas when the Wishbone was developed.) He also was an outstanding punt returner who never averaged less than 10 yards per return in a season, and had a career norm of 12.0.*

Bobby Anderson *(far left) was on his way to becoming the Big 8's most productive quarterback ever until he was moved to full-back his senior year. The move was good for Anderson, who had good size (6-0, 210), a lot of power, and (at the end of his Colorado career) All-America honors. Anderson, the first draft choice of the Broncos in 1970, immediately moved into the lineup opposite Floyd Little. In Anderson's first two years, he helped block Little to two AFC rushing titles. Anderson's best season was 1971, when he ran for 533 yards and made 37 receptions. Injuries took their toll on Anderson and he had to retire after the 1973 season.*

<

Charley Harraway *was just what the Washington Redskins needed throughout the late 1960s—a good, steady running back. Unfortunately, for Harraway at least, he showed up in Washington the same year as Larry Brown. Harraway complemented Brown well. He was a big (6-2, 215) full-back who blocked like a crazy man, ran well, and led the running backs in both the AFL and NFL in receptions in 1969 with 55. After five years with the Redskins, he went to the WFL, a move that immediately affected Brown's statistics. For his career, Harraway ran for 3,019 yards and caught 158 passes.*

MacArthur Lane spent 11 years in the NFL with St. Louis, Green Bay, and Kansas City. He was the man behind the success of each team's running game. In 1970, with St. Louis, the Utah State product was the number-three rusher in the NFL with 977 yards and a league-high 13 touchdowns. Two years later he was traded to Green Bay, where he not only ran for 821 yards (and a 4.6-yard average), but used his power and size (6-1, 230) to help block John Brockington to 1,027 yards. When Lane went to Kansas City in 1975, Brockington virtually disappeared from the NFL rushing lists. But Lane continued his successful play. In 1976, he ran for 542 yards and led the NFL with 66 receptions. He retired in 1978 with career totals of 4,656 rushing yards and 287 receptions.

Jim Kiick wasn't supposed to be a star when the Dolphins drafted him on the fifth round out of Wyoming. After all, the Dolphins had taken Larry Csonka in the first round. But Kiick earned the starting halfback position next to Csonka and led the Dolphins in rushing his first two seasons (1968-69). Kiick's production fell off as Csonka's increased and the Dolphins started using Mercury Morris more frequently. Kiick went to the WFL in 1975 after having gained 3,644 yards and caught 221 passes. He later returned to the NFL for two years, with Denver and Washington.

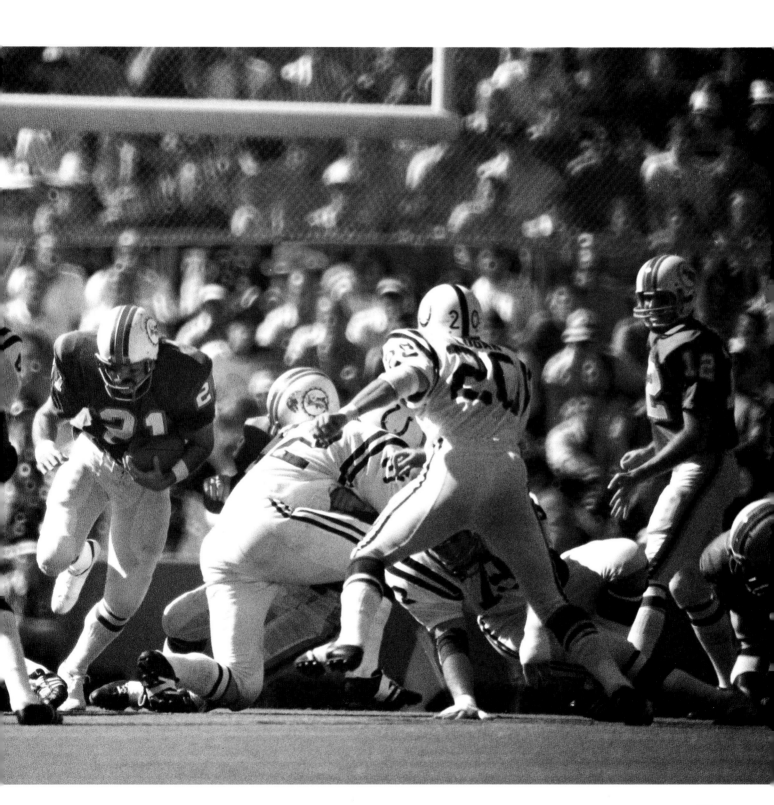

Jim Braxton never received much credit for helping the Buffalo Bills' "Electric Company" offensive line turn loose the Juice (O.J. Simpson). But without Braxton throwing his weight (240 pounds) around, Simpson wouldn't have been nearly as effective. Braxton, out of West Virginia, earned a starting position the same year (1972) Simpson first led the NFL in rushing, and gained 453 yards himself. Three years later, when O.J. again led the NFL, Braxton had his best season, powering for 823 yards and scoring 13 touchdowns. When Simpson was hurt in 1977, Braxton also gave the Bills' passing game a lift, making 43 receptions, second most on the team. He retired after a year (1978) with Miami, having rushed for 2,890 career yards.

It is not a coincidence that **Rocky Bleier's** emergence as a starter in Pittsburgh was the same year as the club's first appearance in the Super Bowl, nor that the Steelers haven't returned since he retired. Bleier had spent four military service-interrupted years with the Steelers (totaling only 70 yards) before he earned a starting job in 1974. In the next seven years, he ran for 3,839 yards, caught 113 passes, and blocked Franco Harris and the Steelers to four Super Bowls. Bleier could be much more than a blocker, however, which he proved in 1976, when he ran for 1,036 yards and a 4.7-yard average.

Roland Harper of Louisiana Tech was drafted by Chicago on the seventeenth round the same year the Bears made Walter Payton their number-one selection. Payton and Harper ended up starting together. Harper's blocking, receiving, and running ability proved almost as important to the Bears as Payton's. Harper had his best year in 1978 with 992 yards, 43 receptions, and eight touchdowns (Payton had 1,395 yards). He missed all of 1979 due to a knee injury, but came back to start in 1980. Harper, who later lost his starting job to Matt Suhey, ranks as the number-four rusher in Chicago history with 3,044 yards.

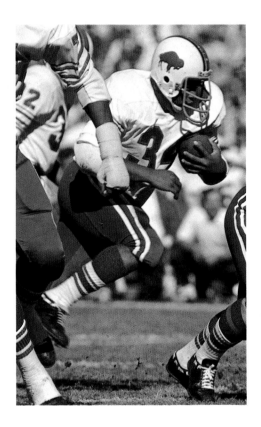

Wayne Morris left SMU as the school's career rushing leader (ahead of Doak Walker, Kyle Rote, and Wayne Maxson), but he has earned his NFL stripes as a blocker and consummate team player. He has blocked for St. Louis record holders Jim Otis, Terry Metcalf, and Ottis Anderson. Yet Morris still can run with authority; in his eight years, he has gained 3,373 yards and has scored a team-record 37 touchdowns. He also holds the St. Louis mark of 36 carries in a game. Morris, who is one of the most dependable ball handlers in the game, once went 180 consecutive carries without a fumble.

When the Saints drafted **Tony Galbreath** of Missouri one round after they had taken Chuck Muncie, a lot of people questioned why a team would want two big fullback-type runners (Galbreath was 6-0, 228). But they both started that year (1976), and Galbreath turned out to be quite a find. In five years with New Orleans, he ran for 2,865 yards and caught 284 passes. In four of his five seasons, he was among the top 10 receivers in the NFC, including ranking second in 1978 with 74 receptions. He was traded to Minnesota in 1981 and has spent much of his time as a third-down specialist behind Ted Brown and Darrin Nelson. In 1983 he ran for 474 yards and had 45 receptions.

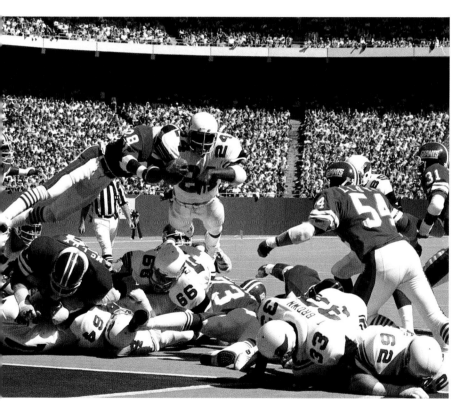

Kenny King has never quite received the notoriety he deserves. As a senior at Oklahoma, he had the best average per carry in the nation (7.8), but was overshadowed by teammate, and Heisman Trophy winner, Billy Sims. As a rookie with the Oilers, he didn't get much of a chance to play as Earl Campbell's backup. Although he has been a starter since being traded to the Raiders in 1980, King has spent much of that time in the shadows of Mark van Eeghen and Marcus Allen. Nevertheless, King, who holds the Super Bowl record for longest reception (80 yards), has gained 2,156 career yards and has distinguished himself as a blocker.

Lynn Cain is yet another USC tailback to play in the NFL. (After a year as a reserve, Cain actually switched positions and set the USC rushing record for fullbacks.) In his second year with the Falcons (1980), he ran for 915 yards as William Andrews's backfield partner. The next season he added 538 yards and 55 receptions. He suffered a severe knee injury, but came back strong the next season. In 1983. the Falcons' extensive use of the one-back formation limited Cain's production, but after five years in the NFL he has rushed for 2,037 yards and made 110 receptions.

Matt Suhey was a four-year starter at Penn State, where he finished as the number-two rusher in school history. Drafted by Chicago in 1980, Suhey earned a starting position in his second season and immediately began posting more than representative numbers. In three years as Walter Payton's running mate, he has run for 1,408 yards, including 681 and a 4.6-yard average in 1983. He also has caught 118 passes and blocked admirably.

THE MONEY MEN

Lest we forget: Football is a team game. Individual statistics are nice, but the real goal is to win. And to win in the playoffs is even better.

NFL history is full of great individuals who never were fortunate enough to play on a team that could make the playoffs, let alone win there. Only once did O. J. Simpson's Buffalo teams advance to the postseason—in 1974, when the Bills were unceremoniously dumped 32-14 by the Pittsburgh Steelers (who were on their way to a victory in Super Bowl IX). On the other hand, many players on championship teams were soon forgotten. The names of Clarence Esser of the 1947 Chicago Cardinals and Eberle Schultz of the 1945 Cleveland Rams, for example, don't pop into the minds of most football fans when recalling the best players they have seen. But they were out there, playing for the NFL championship.

Then there are the great players who have saved some of their best performances for the postseason. Franco Harris will break Jim Brown's career rushing marks in 1984, but he already owns all of the career playoff running records. Similarly, Tony Dorsett has climbed up to the number-eight place on the all-time rushing chart, and is second to Harris in all three major career postseason rushing categories—carries, yards, and touchdowns.

Back in the 1930s, when only two teams made the playoffs, it was more difficult to compile gaudy career marks, but there were some outstanding single-game performances. In the 1947 NFL Championship Game between the Chicago Cardinals and Philadelphia Eagles, there were two. The Cardinals' Elmer Angsman set a playoff record with 159 yards rushing on only 10 carries. Twice he broke loose on Comiskey Park's frozen turf for 70-yard touchdown runs. Chicago's other two scores (the Cardinals won 28-21) were by Charley Trippi, on a 44-yard run and a 75-yard punt return.

Two years later, the Eagles' Steve Van Buren put his name in the record book. In the 1947 game, Van Buren, the NFL's leading rusher that season, had been held to 26 yards by the Cardinals. In 1949, however, in a quagmire at the rain-soaked Coliseum, he shredded the Los Angeles Rams' defense for 196 yards on 31 carries and Philadelphia won the championship 14-0. Van Buren's mark still stands as the NFC Championship Game record.

Doak Walker had two big days in successive (and successful) championship games for Detroit. In 1952, Walker (who had been injured most of the year and hadn't scored at all during the regular season) broke open a 7-0 game with a 67-yard touchdown sprint in the third quarter. The Lions went on to win 17-7. The next year, Walker scored a touchdown in the first quarter and kicked a field goal in the second, as Detroit went ahead 10-3 at halftime. But Cleveland came back to go on top 16-10 in

Alan Ameche's *NFL career is sometimes erroneously thought to have included only one play. After winning the Heisman Trophy at Wisconsin, the big (6-0, 220) fullback joined the Baltimore Colts in 1955. During his six-year career, "The Horse" led the team in rushing five times, including his rookie year, when he topped the entire NFL with 961 yards. Ameche scored the first touchdown on a two-yard run in the* 1958 NFL Championship Game against the New York Giants. Then, at 8:15 of overtime, Ameche cemented his reputation. He barged into the end zone behind the right side of his line for the winning points (23-17) to culminate what has been called "the greatest game ever played." Ameche retired as the Colts' leading career rusher with 4,045 yards.

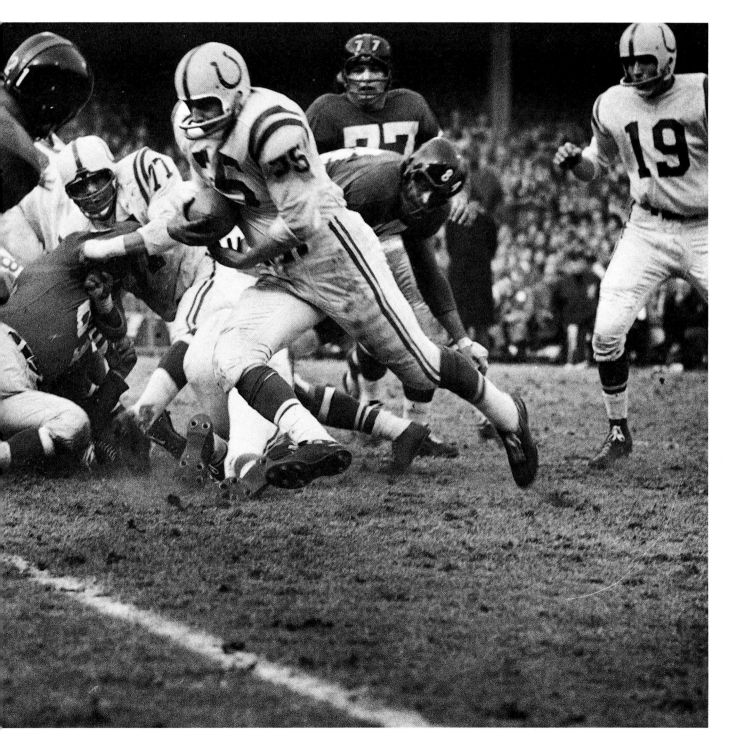

the fourth quarter. When the Lions scored on a 33-yard pass from Bobby Layne to Jim Doran with 2:08 to go in the game, Walker came in to kick the deciding extra point for a 17-16 victory.

The list of great playoff performances is long. But the amazing thing about the playoffs is the number of truly great backs who are remembered almost solely for what they did after the regular season had ended. From Alan Ameche's one play (the winning touchdown run) in the 1958 NFL Championship Game, to John Riggins's four-game 1982 playoff streak that culminated in his record-setting day in Super Bowl XVII,

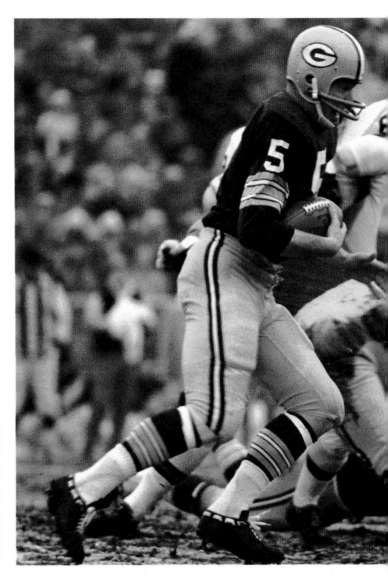

The signing of Heisman Trophy winner **Billy Cannon** of LSU by the Houston Oilers in 1960 was one of the great coups for the newly-formed AFL. He helped lead the Oilers to 10 wins during both the 1960 and 1961 regular seasons and led the AFL in rushing in 1961 (948 yards). His biggest games in those seasons, however, came in the playoffs. In the 1960 AFL Championship Game, the Oilers led 17-16, but the Los Angeles Chargers were making a comeback. Cannon squelched that when he caught a short pass, broke a tackle, and outran the Chargers' defense for an 88-yard touchdown to seal the Oilers' 24-16 victory. In the next season's championship game, Cannon again broke tackles to turn a medium-length reception into a long touchdown. That 35-yard scoring pass from George Blanda was the only touchdown of the game; the Oilers again beat the Chargers, 10-3, for the AFL championship.

Paul Hornung's forte wasn't running the ball, but scoring points. He did everything well in his nine-year career, rushing for 3,711 yards, catching 130 passes, throwing five touchdown passes, and returning kicks for a 24.8-yard average. The Heisman Trophy winner from Notre Dame led the league in scoring three times, including a record 176 points in 1960. He also set the NFL playoff scoring record in the 1961 NFL Championship Game. In a 37-0 victory over the New York Giants, Hornung opened the scoring with a six-yard run, kicked three field goals, and added four PATs for 19 points, a mark that still stands.

single playoff performances have overshadowed entire careers of even some of the best backs in NFL history.

Marcus Allen of the Los Angeles Raiders is the most recent player to enter the public consciousness for his postseason play. Although Allen is one of the most versatile backs in the NFL, his reputation was secured by his record-setting heroics (191 yards) in Super Bowl XVIII. However, for Allen, and so many other fine backs, securing a reputation can mean not only guaranteeing it, but also—in the historical sense—limiting it.

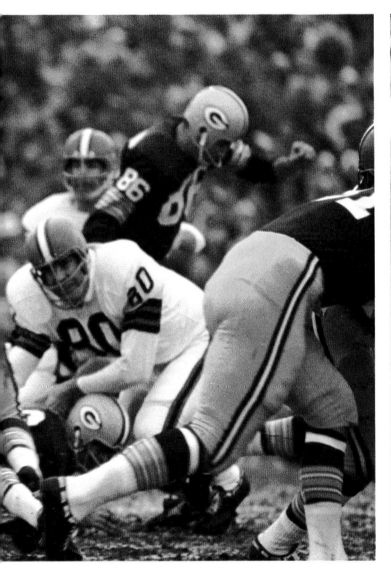

Keith Lincoln was a big-play back during his eight years with the Chargers and the Bills. In his career, he ran for 3,383 yards, caught 165 passes, averaged 26.1 yards on kickoff returns and 13.7 yards on punt returns, and threw five touchdown passes. But Lincoln, a halfback with fullback size (6-1, 217) who was twice named the most valuable player in the AFL All-Star Game, saved his best day for the playoffs. In the 1963 AFL Championship Game (in which the Chargers defeated Boston 51-10), he gained 206 yards on 13 carries (still a championship game record) and caught seven passes for 128 more yards. He scored twice, on a 67-yard run and a 25-yard reception.

Elijah Pitts was one of the great reserves in NFL history. He played 11 years in the NFL, 10 of them with the Packers. He rarely started, but he always contributed. Pitts's best year was 1966, when he gained 393 yards and scored 10 touchdowns. That year, he also started in Super Bowl I against the Kansas City Chiefs. Sharing the ball-carrying duties with Jim Taylor, Pitts helped power the Packers to a 35-10 victory. For the day, he had 11 carries, 45 yards, two touchdowns, and one Super Bowl ring.

Tom Matte had three great playoff games—one as a quarterback and two as a halfback. In 1965, Matte (who had been a quarterback at Ohio State) played for the injured Johnny Unitas in a Western Conference playoff game. Although Matte had the Colts ahead most of the game, the Packers won 13-10 in overtime. Three years later, with Earl Morrall at quarterback, Matte ran for 88 yards and scored an NFL Championship Game-record three touchdowns as the Colts stormed past Cleveland 34-0 and into Super Bowl III. In the Super Bowl Matte again was a star, but in a losing cause. He ran for a record 116 yards on only 11 carries to provide the Colts with most of their offense. When he retired, Matte was the Colts' second-leading career rusher (4,646 yards) and their number-five receiver (249 for 2,869 yards).

Matt Snell was the New York Jets' leading rusher five times in his nine-year (1964-1972) career. His productivity has stood the test of time; he still ranks as the number-two rusher in Jets history (4,285 yards). He also owns the club record for single-game rushing yards (180). But the game he is most remembered for is Super Bowl III. Joe Namath won most valuable player honors that day, but it was Snell who really sparked the Jets. He carried the ball 30 times for 121 yards (both records) and the Jets' only touchdown in their 16-7 victory over the Colts. All day long his slants to the weakside kept the Colts off balance, which allowed Namath to pass successfully.

Ed Podolak was Mr. Versatility in his nine years in Kansas City. He led the Chiefs in rushing five times, in receiving three times, and in punt returns three times. He still ranks as Kansas City's all-time rusher (4,451 yards) and number-three receiver (288 catches). But it was his play in the 27-24 overtime loss to Miami in the 1971 AFC Divisional Playoff Game that made his name with football fans. Podolak scored the Chiefs' first and third touchdowns, and, after Miami scored to tie the game with 1:36 left, returned the ensuing kickoff 78 yards to set up an unsuccessful field goal attempt. Overall, Podolak had an incredible day. He rushed 17 times for 85 yards, caught eight passes for 110, returned three kickoffs for 153, and two punts for 2—a 350-yard total.

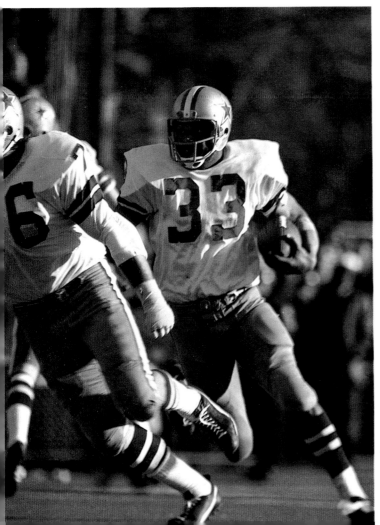

Duane Thomas didn't stay around the NFL long, and the defenders of his day were glad. In 1970, Thomas was rookie of the year after he gained 803 yards. He then ran for 135 yards in a divisional playoff game and 143 in the NFC Championship Game. In Super Bowl V, he scored the Cowboys' only touchdown as they lost to the Colts 16-13. The next year, he again led the Cowboys in rushing with 793 yards. He scored important touchdowns in each of the playoff wins to help lead the Cowboys back to the Super Bowl. In the 24-3 Super Bowl VI victory against the Dolphins—the Cowboys' first NFL title—Thomas led a punishing Dallas ground attack with 95 yards on 19 carries and scored the clinching touchdown. Many considered him the player of the game, an honor that was awarded instead to Cowboys quarterback Roger Staubach.

As **Larry Csonka** went, so went the Miami Dolphins in the early 1970s. Three times Csonka rushed for 1,000 yards in a season, and each time Miami reached the Super Bowl. In Miami's two Super Bowl victories, Csonka was the main man. In Game VII, he ran for 112 yards on only 15 carries and helped set up both Dolphins scores in a 14-7 win over Washington. The next year Csonka broke Matt Snell's Super Bowl records with 33 carries for 145 yards. He also scored twice as the Dolphins beat the Vikings 24-7. Csonka, who played 11 years in the NFL, retired as the number-six rusher in league history with 8,081 yards and 64 touchdowns.

Clarence Davis gained more than 2,200 yards in two years at USC, but most people remember him only as the back who replaced O. J. Simpson there. He had much the same problem getting recognition in the NFL. In eight years with the Oakland Raiders, Davis rushed for 3,640 yards and a sparkling 4.5-yard average and never averaged less than 4.1 yards per carry in a season. He also averaged 27.1 yards on kickoff returns. But Davis's legacy centers around only two games. In a 1974 AFC Divisional Playoff Game, he outfought three Miami defenders to catch a fourth-down, eight-yard touchdown pass from Ken Stabler. The play, with 26 seconds left, gave the Raiders a 28-26 victory. Two years later in Super Bowl XI, Davis gained 137 yards on just 16 carries to spearhead the Raiders to a 32-14 victory over the Vikings.

There is more to **Franco Harris** being the NFL's career playoff rusher than simply his 10 postseason appearances. Harris was the big gun on the ground for the Steelers in each of their four Super Bowl victories. In Pittsburgh's first Super Bowl appearance (Game IX), Harris was named the most valuable player. He broke Larry Csonka's Super Bowl records with 34 carries and 158 yards as the Steelers defeated the Vikings 16-6. The next year,

Harris was the game's leading ground gainer again, bulling for 82 yards in the Steelers' 21-17 defeat of the Cowboys. In Super Bowl XII, he ran for 68 yards, including a fourth-quarter score that broke open a tight game and led to a 35-31 victory over Dallas. In the Steelers' last Super Bowl victory (31-19 over the Rams in Game XIV), Harris was held to 46 yards, but scored two touchdowns, including the game-clincher in the fourth quarter.

Preston Pearson was a solid, versatile running back for 14 years in the NFL. He ran for 3,609 yards and caught 254 passes. But those numbers pale compared to his playoff statistics. Pearson not only shares the record for most appearances in the Super Bowl, he did it with three different teams (Baltimore in Super Bowl III, Pittsburgh in Game IX, and Dallas in Super Bowls X, XII, and XIII). His biggest game helped put the Cowboys into the

Super Bowl. In the 1975 NFC Championship Game, he caught seven passes for 123 yards and a record three touchdowns as the wild card Cowboys defeated the favored Los Angeles Rams 37-7.

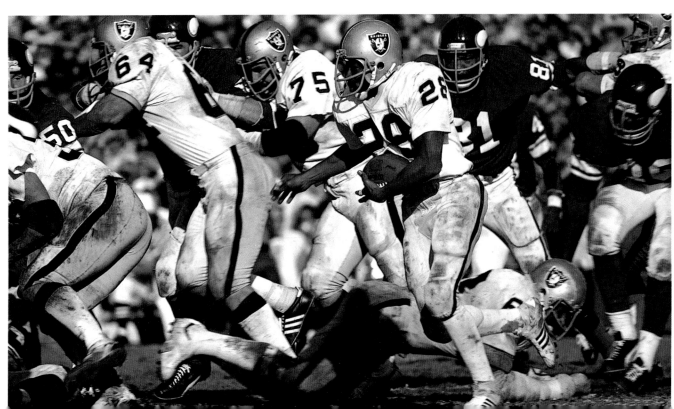

Wendell Tyler frequently is thought of as a small runner who gains his yards outside. He is quick, but he is not as undersized (5-10, 200) as many think, and he has the strength and stamina to take on the middle of an opposing defense. In his seven years in the NFL, he has gained 4,122 yards. Tyler also has a lot of determination. In Super Bowl XIV, he was knocked out of the game three times by exceptionally hard hits from the Steelers. But each time, Tyler re-entered the game to carry the Rams' rushing attack. He finished with a game-high 60 yards and three receptions for 20 more.

< The Tampa Bay Buccaneers chose **Ricky Bell** over Tony Dorsett in the 1977 draft, and the All-America from USC in turn became the franchise's career rushing leader (with 3,057 yards). Bell was the force on the ground for four years for Tampa Bay, and his best year paralleled that of the Buccaneers. In 1979, he gained 1,263 yards to take the Buccaneers to the playoffs. Then, in the NFC Divisional Playoff Game against Philadelphia, he set a postseason record with 38 carries, on which he gained 142 yards. Bell's two touchdowns paced the 24-17 victory.

The 1982 season was shortened by a players' strike, but it still was a good year for **Freeman McNeil** of the Jets. McNeil, an All-America at UCLA, led the NFL in rushing with 786 yards. (His 5.2-yard average also was tops in the league.) Then, in an AFC playoff game against Cincinnati, he ran for 202 yards on 21 carries, the second most yards in playoff history. He also demonstrated his versatility against the Bengals by throwing a 14-yard touchdown pass. The next week, McNeil gained 101 yards on 23 carries as the Jets upset the Raiders in Los Angeles.

In the 1982 playoffs, the Redskins rode "The Diesel," **John Riggins,** to the Super Bowl. Riggins, who earlier in his career had had three 1,000-yard seasons, made the most of his first playoff appearance. For four consecutive games, he gained more than 100 yards (for a playoff record of 610). In the first round against Detroit, he ran for 119 yards. The next week he gained 185 yards on 37 carries and almost single handedly led the Redskins to a 21-7 win against Minnesota. In the NFC Championship Game, Riggins scored twice and gained 140 yards. And in Super Bowl XVII, he set records with 38 carries and 166 yards, ran for the winning fourth-quarter touchdown, and was named the game's most valuable player.

Marcus Allen just might become the first player ever to rush for 1,000 yards and catch 100 passes in the same season. Allen was the Heisman Trophy winner at USC, running for an NCAA-record 2,342 yards in 1981. He was named rookie of the year in the NFL in 1982, after he rushed for 697 yards and caught 38 passes in only nine games. The next year he rushed for 1,014 yards and made 68 receptions. But his biggest game so far was Super Bowl XVIII. On only 20 carries, Allen ran for a record 191 yards, including the longest run in Super Bowl history (74 yards). He also caught two passes, scored twice, set four Super Bowl records, tied two more, and was named the game's most valuable player.

SHOOTING STARS

*Early in 1968, **Paul Robinson** was a little-known, third-round draft choice from Arizona who was going to the expansion Cincinnati Bengals. By the end of the season, he was the AFL's leading rusher (1,023 yards on a league-high 238 carries). Robinson was only the second back (Beattie Feathers was the first) to gain 1,000 yards in his first year of professional football. Although he had several other successful seasons, Robinson never again equaled his rookie output. He finished his six-year career with 2,947 yards.*

When Beattie Feathers broke onto the NFL scene in 1934, he seemed destined for a sprint straight to the Hall of Fame. The All-America from Tennessee moved into a starting position in a Chicago Bears' lineup that already included eventual Hall of Famers Bronko Nagurski, George Musso, and Link Lyman. He took most of the ball-carrying duties away from Nagurski and Gene Ronzani, and reduced the great Jack Manders to a blocking back. He immediately shattered the NFL rushing record as he became the first back to gain 1,000 yards in a season (1,004 on only 101 carries).

But Feathers never made the Hall of Fame. He gained a total of only 975 yards on 259 carries in the last six years of his seven-season NFL career, including two years spent as a benchwarmer for the NFL's old Brooklyn Dodgers. He retired after spending a season with Green Bay, for whom he netted 21 yards.

Feathers's story is not unusual. NFL history is dotted with players who have enjoyed a successful year and then, seemingly, disappeared. Conversely, there also were those who, in the midst of a long and mediocre career, had one brief, shining moment.

In 1950, Bill Grimes of Green Bay set the NFL record by averaging 16.7 yards per carry in a game (10 attempts, 167 yards) against the New York Yanks. In the rest of his three-year NFL career, Grimes gained 495 yards on 135 attempts, or 3.7 yards per carry.

The obvious question is Why? If players are talented enough to be so successful once, why doesn't that success continue? What is it that is so magical for them for that one season, one game, or even one play?

The answers, of course, are plentiful. Injuries is the most obvious. Take the example of Greg Cook, who led the AFL in passing in 1969 when he was rookie of the year. That year the league also included John Hadl, Len Dawson, Daryle Lamonica, Joe Namath, Bob Griese, and Jack Kemp. They all had memorable careers. But whatever happened to Cook? He hurt his arm, was never effective again, and eventually ended up being replaced in succession by Virgil Carter and young Ken Anderson (who never would have been drafted by the Bengals if Cook had stayed healthy).

The personnel surrounding a player also can contribute to a sudden demise. John Brockington appeared as if he could run through anything for four years with the Green Bay Packers; then he declined into a three-yards-per-carry back. But Brockington didn't have to shoulder the entire blame for his dwindling statistics. He was helped down the ladder of success by the retirements of all-pro guard Gale Gillingham and long-time center Ken Bowman, and by the trade of blocker *par excellence* MacArthur Lane.

A player's own attitude and desire can have a lot to do with his success, or lack of it. There hasn't been a more talented running back than Duane Thomas, but he didn't make things easy for himself. After two brilliant, but troubled, years with the Cowboys (he was the leading rusher in Super Bowl VI), he was traded to the Patriots, then back to the Cowboys, then to the Chargers, and, finally, to the Redskins, whom he was with for several relatively unproductive seasons.

Coaching changes, losing starting status, and age can be other factors that lend to the here today-gone tomorrow syndrome. Unfortunately, so can tragedy. Joe Delaney of Kansas City looked like he might be a long-term NFL star in his first two seasons (1981-82), but his untimely death between the 1982 and 1983 seasons took from the NFL one of its most prized backs and individuals.

There are many players who either don't make it in the NFL at all or don't ever get a chance to shine. The shooting stars at least had their moments.

Although many backs in the last 50 years have gained more yards in a season than **Beattie Feathers** *did in 1934 (1,004), in many ways no one has matched his accomplishment. No rushing record has had the longevity (13 years) of Feathers's mark. And his 9.94-yard average still is way ahead of the second-best qualifying average of all time, 6.87 yards per carry by quarterback Bobby Douglass of the Bears in 1972. Feathers never did match his rookie yardage again. In his last six years, he gained only 975 yards total.*

Before knee injuries wrecked his career, **Junior Coffey** had shown opposing coaches enough for them to consider him one of the best young talents in the NFL. Coffey was selected by Atlanta in the expansion draft after playing with Green Bay as a rookie. Each of the next two years (1966 and 1967), he gained 722 yards rushing. If he could do that for the hapless Falcons, it was reasoned, he would tear up the league playing for anybody else. But all he tore up in 1968 was a knee. His return to the NFL with the New York Giants was aborted by another injury.

In 1966, Buffalo's **Bobby Burnett,** a fourth-round draft choice from Arkansas, earned AFL rookie of the year honors, beating out Kansas City's Mike Garrett. Burnett ran for 766 yards, caught 34 passes for 419 more, and was selected to play in the AFL All-Star Game. But injuries held him to 96 yards in 1967, knocked him out of 1968 altogether, and limited him to five carries for nine yards with Denver in his last season (1969).

>

Willie Ellison played in the NFL for eight years and collected 3,426 rushing yards. In many senses, however, he was a one-game player. Ellison played in the shadows of Dick Bass, Tommy Mason, and Les Josephson the first four years of his Los Angeles Rams career, even though he did replace the injured Josephson in 1968 and gain 616 yards. In 1971, Ellison became a starter and netted 1,000 yards on 211 attempts. The highlight of the year was a late-season date against New Orleans in which Ellison set the NFL single-game record by rushing for 247 yards (on 26 carries). Ellison again led the Rams in rushing in 1972, but then finished his career in obscurity with the Chiefs.

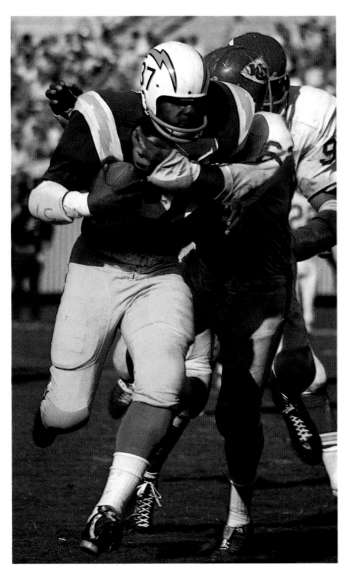

The possibility of a healthy **Andy Livingston** in the same backfield with a healthy Gale Sayers probably gave opposing defenses pause in the mid-1960s. But Livingston, even more so than Sayers, couldn't escape the injury jinx in his NFL career. Little used as a rookie, the bruising (6-1, 234) fullback from Phoenix College teamed with Sayers in 1965 and averaged 5.8 yards per carry.

An injury cost him all of 1966, however, and when he returned he could produce only 66 yards on 35 carries the next two seasons. Given new life in New Orleans in 1969, Livingston set a Saints record with 761 yards rushing, caught 28 passes, and made the Pro Bowl. The next year injuries struck again, and he retired with a career total of 1,216 yards rushing.

The San Diego Chargers thought they had built a backfield for the next decade in 1967, when they unveiled halfback Dickie Post and fullback **Brad Hubbert,** who finished fourth and fifth in the league in rushing, respectively. The Chargers turned out only to be half right. Post went on to lead the AFL in rushing in 1969, and Hubbert, who had been rookie of the year, went on to oblivion. In 1967, Hubbert gained 643 yards and had a league-leading 5.5-yard average. Injuries forced him to miss all but two games of 1968; he never recovered and left the Chargers in 1970. His career statistics showed 1,270 yards and only a 3.7-yard average after his rookie year.

Nobody knew much about rookie **Don Woods** when the Chargers obtained him in 1974. He had been cut by Green Bay, but the former New Mexico quarterback earned a starting position with San Diego and went on to finish second in the NFL in rushing with 1,162 yards and a 5.1-yard average. His best day came in the third week when he rushed for 157 yards against Miami, including a 56-yard touchdown. Woods was named AFC rookie of the year. The Chargers kept hoping for a repeat performance from the 6-foot 2-inch, 208-pounder. They never got it. Woods couldn't average better than 3.6-yards-per-carry for San Diego again, and finished his career with the San Francisco 49ers.

Terdell Middleton came from nowhere in 1978 to gain 1,116 yards, catch 34 passes, and score 12 touchdowns for Green Bay. The next year, he returned to nowhere again. Middleton had gained only 97 yards as a rookie out of Memphis State in 1977. After his big year, his production dropped off, and in his last five years in the NFL (1979-1983) he gained a total of 835 yards (a 3.5-yard average).

Woody Green joined the Chiefs in 1974 after one of the most fabulous college football careers ever; he had gained 3,806 yards and been a two-time consensus All-America at Arizona State. But injuries tormented Green in his NFL career. He missed four games as a rookie with a collarbone injury, but still led Kansas City in rushing with 509 yards. The next year, he again led the Chiefs in rushing (611 yards), even though he missed two games with a dislocated knee. Green's career was ended in 1976 by another knee injury.

The Seattle Seahawks might have made the playoffs earlier in the club's history if **David Sims** hadn't been forced to retire. Sims was a big (6-3, 216) back from Georgia Tech who joined the Seahawks in 1977. He became a starter in his second season and gained 752 yards, caught 30 passes, and led the NFL with 15 touchdowns despite missing four games with a knee injury. Sims started the 1979 season, but had to retire early in the year due to a serious neck injury.

Terry Miller's rushing totals look like an inverse pyramid. The All-America from Oklahoma State finished his college career as the number-four rusher in NCAA history with 4,582 yards. The Buffalo Bills made him their first draft pick in 1978 and he validated their choice by gaining 1,060 yards. But Miller (5-10, 196) wasn't built to stand the pounding in the NFL. In his second year, he gained only 484 yards and his average dropped from 4.5 yards to 3.5 yards. In his last two seasons, spent with the Bills and Seahawks, he managed only 39 yards on 14 carries.

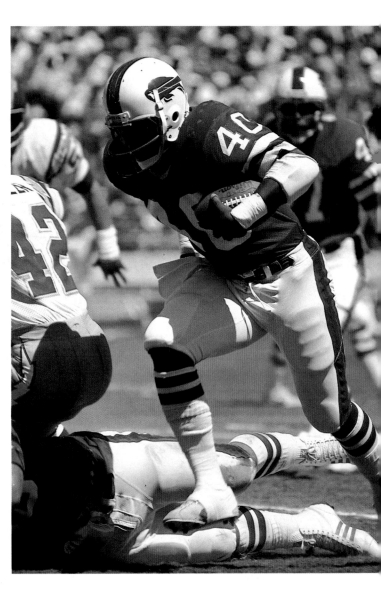

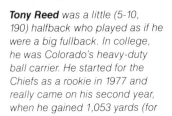

Tony Reed was a little (5-10, 190) halfback who played as if he were a big fullback. In college, he was Colorado's heavy-duty ball carrier. He started for the Chiefs as a rookie in 1977 and really came on his second year, when he gained 1,053 yards (for a 5.1-yard average) and caught 48 passes. A knee injury the next year cut Reed's season in half (when he had 446 yards and 34 receptions). He never fully recovered from the injury and finished his career with Denver in 1981.

Joe Delaney *was one of the briefest but brightest flashes in NFL history, not only on the field, but off. A product of Northwest Louisiana State, Delaney was chosen by Kansas City in the second round of the 1981 draft. He was selected AFC rookie of the year and played in the AFC-NFC Pro Bowl after gaining 1,121 yards for a 4.8-yard average. Delaney was hampered by injuries and an eye problem his second season, but still led the Chiefs in rushing. He tragically drowned prior to the 1983 season attempting to save three young children from the same fate.*

THE CRAFTSMEN

Even the most casual pro football fans mention Jim Brown, Gale Sayers, and O.J. Simpson when they talk about running backs. Those with longer memories will add Hugh McElhenny or Lenny Moore. Although much of NFL legend is based on such players, the day-to-day action—the pounding, hitting, and sweating—is dominated by another breed of runner.

For every Pro Football Hall of Fame running back, there are hundreds of others in the NFL who are not quite so talented, not quite so productive, or not quite so fortunate. But they are the backs who carry the ball, catch the passes, and do the blocking in most of the games. Only one player who was playing running back in 1968 (Gale Sayers) is in the Hall of Fame. That does not imply, however, that there were no outstanding backs in pro football at that time; rather, just that some of the best football players don't always get long-term (or even short-term) recognition.

The yards a running back gains, the publicity he receives, or even the amount of time he plays aren't necessarily accurate indicators of his ability, desire, or importance. Rob Carpenter, for example, might have been just another faceless name, just a little-used backup for Earl Campbell, "just a guy" as the saying in the NFL goes. However, the Oilers traded Carpenter to the New York Giants, and he became a full-fledged NFL star. Suddenly he had talent, power, a nose for the end zone. He had those qualities all along, of course, but he wasn't in the situation to show them off.

Carpenter was lucky; he got the chance to display his wares. Many backs never do. Rob Scribner earned a position as a running back with the Rams in 1973 despite having been a second-string quarterback at UCLA the year before. He played four years in Los Angeles, gaining 361 yards on an outstanding 4.9-yards-per-carry average. But he never got a chance to start because backfield mate Lawrence McCutcheon was setting Rams rushing records. It is easy for those who saw Scribner play to visualize him as the toast of Atlanta, or Kansas City, or New York, if he had been with the Falcons, or Chiefs, or Giants.

Even when many backs do get a chance to play, and even when they are successful, they suffer by comparison to the "name" players of the day. They don't get the credit they deserve while they are playing, and they are forgotten soon after they call it a career. Mel Farr and Dickie Post, for instance, were phenomenal backs, with a capital P. They both entered pro football in 1967, Farr with Detroit of the NFL, and Post with San Diego of the AFL. Farr was among the league rushing leaders and was named rookie of the year. Post was fourth in the AFL in rushing as a rookie, and improved his totals each of the next several years, until he led the AFL in rushing in 1969. Both are rarely remembered anymore.

*It would be easy to understand why **Bob Hoernschemeyer** frequently is forgotten, since he played in the same Detroit backfield as Bobby Layne, Doak Walker, and Pat Harder. Except that in each of his first four years with the team, it was Hoernschemeyer who led the Lions in rushing. "Hunchy," as he was called, was a multi-dimensional back who played his college ball at Indiana. In his 10-year career (with four AAFC or NFL teams), he played tailback, halfback, fullback, wingback, and defensive back—and he played each position well. He passed for 4,302 yards and 42 touchdowns, rushed for 4,548 yards, made 109 receptions, averaged 12.1 yards on punt returns and 25.2 yards on kickoff returns, and scored 39 touchdowns.*

The NFL annals are full of running backs (and other positions, as well) who cut a wide swath through the league for several years. "Guys" who were solid, productive, accomplished backs; who were team leaders, sometimes even league leaders. John Brockington led the NFL in rushing as a rookie in 1971 and became the first back to gain more than 1,000 yards the first three years of his career. But who remembers that now?

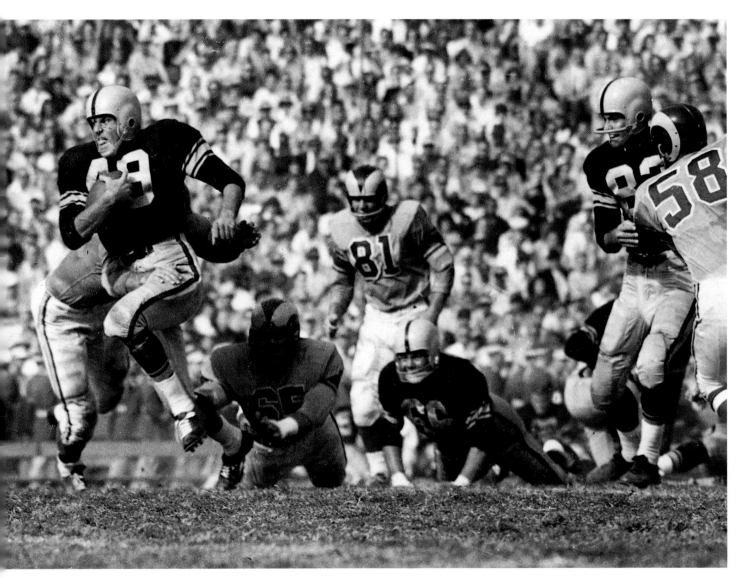

Lynn Chandnois was one of those great backs who labors in obscurity forced upon him by a weak team. An All-America at Michigan State, he played seven years (1950-56) with the Pittsburgh Steelers, during which time the club never had a record better than 6-6. Chandnois could do everything, but he really exceled at kickoff returns. He led the NFL in 1951 with a 32.5-yard average, and the next year set a league record of 35.2 yards per return. Chandnois had his best season in 1953, when he ran for 470 yards, caught 43 passes, and averaged 29 yards per kickoff return. He retired as Pittsburgh's number-two career rusher and still is the number-two kickoff returner in NFL history (29.6-yard average).

Just because most of these players are gone today, because they make their careers doing something other than flashing through a quick-opening hole, storming into the line, or springing another back with a devastating block, doesn't mean they still aren't a part of the NFL heritage. They should be remembered as such. The diligent, dependable workers, the yeomen of the backfield, even more than the few all-time greats, are the ones who made (and continue to make) pro football America's sport.

Mel Triplett was the fullback for the New York Giants when the club played in three NFL Championship Games in a four-year (1956-59) period. He represented power up the middle (he was 6-1, 215) even more than Alex Webster, and led the Giants in rushing in 1960 (573 yards). The next year, he was picked up by the expansion Minnesota Vikings and averaged 5.1 yards behind a makeshift line. He retired after the 1962 season with 2,856 career rushing yards.

Johnny Olszewski *spent much of his 10-year career lining up next to Charley Trippi, Ollie Matson, and Joe Childress. But "Johnny O" didn't have to take a backseat to anyone. In 1959, his second season in Washington after five years with the Chicago Cardinals, he led the NFL with a 6.6-yard average. For his career, the former California All-America ran for 3,320 yards and made 104 receptions.*

Tom (The Bomb) Tracy *played his first two seasons with Detroit, but his career didn't really take off until 1958, when he joined the Pittsburgh Steelers. That season he teamed with Bobby Layne (also coming from Detroit) to take the Steelers to their second-best record ever at that time (7-4-1). Tracy led Pittsburgh in rushing three consecutive years (1958-* *1960)—before John Henry Johnson joined the backfield. Tracy was a compact (5-9, 205) Tennessee product who finished his nine-year career with 2,912 yards, 31 touchdowns, and a reputation as the best halfback-pass artist in the NFL. He completed 24 passes for 854 yards, a 35.6-yards-per-completion average, and six touchdowns.*

>

The Los Angeles Rams made a popular move when they drafted USC halfback **Jon Arnett** in 1957. Arnett paid back the Rams with more than fan appeasement, however. As a rookie, he led the NFL in kickoff returns. The next year Arnett topped the league in punt returns, ran for 683 yards, and caught 35 passes. "Jaguar Jon" played with the Rams for seven years (making the Pro Bowl five times), before finishing his career with three productive seasons in Chicago. He retired in 1966 with career totals of 3,833 rushing yards, 222 receptions, 39 touchdowns, and a 24.7-yard kickoff return average.

<

For the first several seasons of his nine-year career, **Nick Pietrosante** was about all the offense the Detroit Lions had. Pietrosante was the NFL's rookie of the year in 1959, and gained more than 800 yards rushing each of the next two seasons. The big (6-1, 220) fullback pounded out enough yardage in his seven years with the Lions to retire as Detroit's career rushing leader (3,933 yards). He finished his career as a reserve with Cleveland.

Ronnie Bull spent many years running up the middle for the Chicago Bears so that a couple of flashy runners named Willie Galimore and Gale Sayers could run outside. Bull didn't have the ideal size for a fullback—he was 6-0, 200—but he played the position well. In 10 years (including his final season, which was with Philadelphia) he ran for 3,222 yards. Bull was incredibly consistent and gained between 300 and 500 yards seven times. His most productive season was 1968, when he took over for the injured Sayers and gained 472 yards.

Prentice Gautt was one of a series of tough, bruising backs the Cardinals had in the 1960s (along with Joe Childress, John David Crow, Bill Triplett, Willis Crenshaw, Johnny Roland, and Cid Edwards). Obtained from Cleveland in 1961, Gautt led the Cardinals in rushing in his first season with the club. Statistically, however, his best year was his last—1967, when he gained 573 yards. Gautt retired after eight years with 2,466 yards.

Les Josephson didn't make the Dallas Cowboys' squad after signing as a free agent out of Augustana College in 1964. He did, however, go on to play 10 years for the Los Angeles Rams and become the club's number-three career rusher (3,407 yards and a 4.3-yard average). Josephson's best year was 1967, when, joining Dick Bass in the backfield, he gained 800 yards, made 37 receptions, and scored eight touchdowns. He missed the next season with an Achilles tendon injury, but returned to start three more years. In 1970, "Josie" gained 640 yards and caught 44 passes, despite playing with a broken jaw.

Donny Anderson was one of college football's greatest all-purpose backs when he was at Texas Tech. In nine years with Green Bay and St. Louis, he fulfilled the same function. Anderson was a starter in 1967 when the Packers won Super Bowl II. In two of the next three seasons, he led them in rushing. His best season was 1970, when he had 853 yards rushing and made 36 receptions. Anderson was traded to St. Louis in 1972 and twice led the club in rushing. He finished his career with 4,696 rushing yards, 209 receptions, and 56 touchdowns.

Dave Osborn came into the NFL quietly (a thirteenth-round draft choice from North Dakota) and left quietly (retiring after 11 years with the Vikings and 1 with the Packers). His actions spoke loudly, though. Osborn didn't have great size (6-0, 208), but his toughness and consistency were significant reasons why Minnesota dominated the NFC Central during the 1970s. Osborn was second in the NFL in rushing in 1967 with 972 yards and a 4.5-yard average. He missed most of the next season, but came back to regain his starting job and to earn selection to the AFC-NFC Pro Bowl in 1971. He finished his career with 4,336 rushing yards, 173 receptions, 36 touchdowns, and three Super Bowl appearances (Games IV, VIII, and IX).

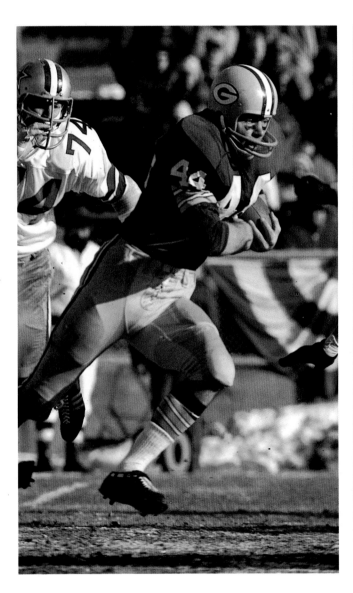

The St. Louis Cardinals drafted **Johnny Roland** of Missouri as a "future" in 1965. He proved worth waiting for. As a rookie in 1966, Roland led the Cardinals with 695 yards. The next season, he finished fourth in the NFL with 876 yards and also caught 20 passes and scored 11 touch-downs. Roland spent seven years with St. Louis, during which time he became the franchise's all-time rusher (3,608 yards on 962 carries). He was selected to play in two Pro Bowls. Today he is an assistant coach with the Chicago Bears.

Pete Banaszak was around whenever the Oakland Raiders needed him. Much of his career he was a reserve, but Banaszak could—and did—step in as a starter and produce. In his sec-ond season (1967) out of Miami, Banaszak replaced the injured Clem Daniels and led the AFL in average per carry (5.5 yards). Four years later, he gained 563 yards and scored eight touch-downs. In 1975, he led the Raid-ers with 672 yards and paced the NFL with 16 rushing touchdowns. In Super Bowl XI, he scored twice. For his career, Banaszak gained 3,772 yards and scored a Raiders' record 47 touchdowns rushing.

> If injuries hadn't cut short his
brilliant career, little (5-9, 190)
dynamo **Dickie Post** might be
remembered as one of pro football's greatest runners. As a
rookie from the University of
Houston with San Diego in 1967,
Post was fourth in the AFL in
rushing with 663 yards. He also
had 32 receptions. The next year,
he finished fifth in rushing and led AFL ballcarriers in yards per
attempt (5.0). Post led the AFL in
rushing in 1969 with 873 yards
and was selected for his second
AFL All-Star Game. A knee injury
put Post on the sidelines for
much of 1970; he retired in 1971
after playing with Denver and
Houston. Post's career totals included 2,605 rushing yards and
96 receptions.

Mel Farr did it all for Detroit in
1967. The All-America speedster
and first-round draft choice from
UCLA had a part in almost everything the Lions' offense did. He
ran for 860 yards (then the second-highest total in Detroit history), caught 39 passes, and
played in the Pro Bowl. He started off just as hot the next
year, but was injured midway
through the season. Farr played
seven seasons with the Lions; in
none of them was he completely
healthy. He retired in 1973 as the
number-two rusher (3,072 yards)
and touchdown scorer (36) in
Lions history.

Emerson Boozer was overlooked much of his career because he played in the same backfield as Matt Snell. Yet Boozer still is the Jets' career rushing leader (5,104 yards) and the number-two touchdown scorer (64). Boozer was a 1966 number-six draft choice from Maryland State who earned a starting position as a rookie. He had nine consecutive seasons with more than 440 yards, led the Jets in rushing three times (including a personal-high 831 yards in 1973), and topped the NFL in touchdowns in 1972.

Charlie Smith proved to be a more-than-adequate replacement for all-time AFL rushing leader Clem Daniels. Smith became a starter for Oakland as a rookie out of Utah in 1968 and averaged 5.3 yards per carry. For four of the next five years (he missed most of one season with an injury), he gained at least 600 yards. In little more than six full seasons, Smith gained 3,351 yards, made 141 receptions, and scored 34 touchdowns. He played in four championship games.

Essex Johnson was an original member of the Cincinnati Bengals. He waited more than three years for a starting opportunity, then made the most of it. In 1971, Johnson, who played his college ball at Grambling, led the AFC with a 6.1-yard average. The next two seasons he led the Bengals in rushing, including a personal-high 997 yards (on a 5.1-yard average) in 1973. A knee injury sidelined Johnson for most of 1974. He played his final season with another expansion team, Tampa Bay, in 1976. Johnson finished his career with 3,236 yards and 146 receptions.

Altie Taylor played in the same backfield as MacArthur Lane at Utah State. All the talent wasn't Lane's, however, as the squat (5-10, 200) Taylor proved in seven seasons with Detroit. Taylor earned a starting position midway through his rookie season (1969) and never gained less than 532 yards in his Detroit career. He joined the Houston Oilers in 1976 after leading the Lions in rushing three times and becoming the club's career rushing leader with 4,297 yards.

Jess Phillips didn't look like he'd be around pro football long after a rookie year with Cincinnati (1968) in which he ran for only seven yards. But Phillips went on to play in the NFL 10 years with four different teams. He led the Bengals in rushing in 1969 and 1970, led the New Orleans Saints in rushing in 1973 (with a personal-high 663 yards), and was a valuable reserve (who averaged 4.7 yards per carry) with the Oakland Raiders in 1975. Phillips retired after two seasons with the New England Patriots with a career total of 3,568 rushing yards.

For the first four years of his career, it looked like **John Brockington** was the replacement for Jim Taylor that Green Bay had so desperately wanted. The big (6-1, 225) fullback from Ohio State led the NFC in rushing as a rookie in 1971 with 1,105 yards (a 5.1-yard average). He then became the first player in NFL history to gain more than 1,000 yards in each of his first three seasons (1,027 in 1972 and 1,144 in 1973). He also was selected to the Pro Bowl after each of those seasons. In 1974, Brockington slipped to 883 yards, but had a personal-high 43 receptions. With the trade of blocker MacArthur Lane and the retirement of half of the offensive line, Brockington's statistics dipped to well under half of their former total. He retired in 1977, after playing a year with Kansas City, with 5,185 career rushing yards.

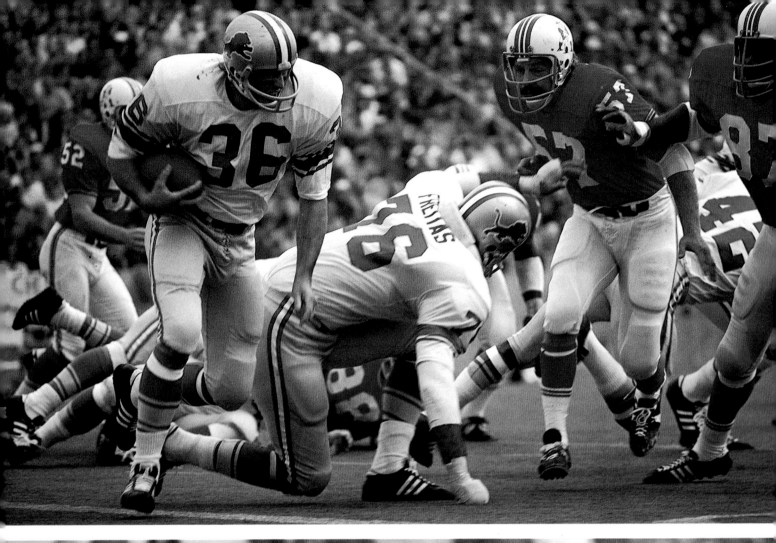

Steve Owens was the picture of durability when he was on his way to winning the Heisman Trophy at Oklahoma. As a junior, the big (6-2, 215) tailback set an NCAA record with 357 carries (61 more than the old record). The next year he had 358 attempts (including 55 against Oklahoma State) and paced the nation with 1,523 yards and 23 touchdowns. But with Detroit, Owens had only one injury-free season. In 1971 (his second year), Owens set Lions records with 246 carries and 1,035 yards. He also caught 32 passes, scored 10 touchdowns, and was selected to the Pro Bowl. Owens finished his five-year career in 1974 with 2,451 yards.

To say **Carl Garrett** had an up-and-down career would be an understatement. The running back from New Mexico Highlands played in a new city almost every other season, and regularly would have an outstanding year followed by a mediocre one. Garrett received AFL rookie of the year mention with Boston in 1969, when he ran for 691 yards (a league-high 5.0-yard average), caught 26 passes, and averaged 28.3 yards on kickoff returns. He dropped to only 272 yards in 1970, but came back for 784 when the Patriots moved to Foxboro. He continued his good-year, bad-year pattern with Chicago, the New York Jets, and Oakland. He retired in 1977 with 4,197 rushing yards, 182 receptions, a 24.7-yard kickoff return average, and 35 touchdowns.

In 1969, one year after being an All-America at Michigan, **Ron Johnson** started next to Leroy Kelly at Cleveland. The next year the Browns traded Johnson to the New York Giants for wide receiver Homer Jones. Johnson had three productive, and three injury-plagued, seasons in New York. In 1970, he gained 1,027 yards (on an NFL-high 263 carries), caught 48 passes, and scored 12 touchdowns. Two years later, he ran for 1,182 yards (again, on an NFL-high 298 carries), caught 45 passes, and scored a league-leading 14 touchdowns. Johnson finished his seven-year career with 4,307 rushing yards, 213 receptions, and 55 touchdowns. He remains the number-two rusher in Giants history.

The timing was not right for **Robert Newhouse.** As a senior at the University of Houston he ran for 1,757 yards, the second most at that time in NCAA history. But no one heard much about Newhouse, because that was the year Ed Marinaro (yards), Lydell Mitchell (touchdowns), and Greg Pruitt (yards per carry) set NCAA single-season marks. The brawny (5-10, 219) Newhouse was drafted by Dallas, where he started at fullback for seven years. But many of his accomplishments were overlooked then because of the play of Calvin Hill and Tony Dorsett. In 1976, Newhouse led the Cowboys in rushing with 930 yards. Newhouse retired before the 1984 season with 4,784 career yards.

The term "flirted with 1,000 yards" must have been developed for **Dave Hampton,** a swift runner from Wyoming. Hampton spent more of his career hovering around the 1,000-yard mark than he'd care to remember. In 1972, after three years as a reserve and a valuable kick returner in Green Bay, Hampton was traded to Atlanta. In the final minutes of the season, he gained six yards to go over the 1,000-yard mark. However, he then was dropped for a six-yard loss on a subsequent play and finished the season with 995 yards. The next year, despite 16 carries in the final quarter of the final game of the season, he again came up just short—this time with 997 yards. Finally, in the last game of 1975, Hampton broke the 1,000-yard barrier and finished with 1,002. Hampton retired in 1976 (after a year in Philadelphia) with 4,512 yards. The 3,490 yards he had gained in Atlanta made him the leading rusher in Falcons history.

Boobie Clark was supposed to be nothing more than training camp fodder when Cincinnati selected him out of Bethune-Cookman on the twelfth round of the 1973 draft. But the big (6-2, 245) fullback went on to be named rookie of the year after he gained 988 yards, caught 45 passes, and scored eight touchdowns. Although injuries sidelined him for part of his second year, Clark returned to lead the Bengals in rushing twice. In 1976 he not only ran for 671 yards, he caught 42 passes for 771 yards, an amazing (at least for a running back) 18.7-yard average. Clark played two years in Houston, where his career was prematurely ended by knee injuries. He had 3,032 rushing yards and 176 receptions.

Delvin Williams currently is one of only two players to hold the season rushing record for two different NFL teams (John Riggins is the other). Williams, who had been a second-round draft choice from Kansas, led San Francisco in rushing from 1975-77. He set the club record with 1,203 yards in 1976. Williams was traded to the Dolphins before the 1978 season and responded with a Miami-record 1,258 yards. He again led the Dolphins in rushing in 1980, the fifth time he had been his team's leading rusher in seven years. Williams finished his career in 1981 (with the Packers), with a combined total 5,598 yards and two Pro Bowl appearances.

*Although he lost his starting job to James Jones in 1983, **Dexter Bussey** remains Detroit's career rushing leader. The eleventh-year player from Texas-Arlington earned a starting position in his second season (1975) and proceeded to lead the Lions in rushing four of the next five years; he gained a career-high 924 yards in 1978. In 1983, Bussey set the Lions' record for career rushing attempts (1,171). He has averaged 4.3 yards per carry in gaining 5,014 yards.*

Otis Armstrong spent much of his career as one of former Denver coach Red Miller's alternating running backs. When he did get the opportunity to play full-time, he showed his real mettle. An All-America at Purdue and Denver's first draft choice in 1973, Armstrong missed most of his rookie season with an injury. In 1974, he became the only player to break O.J. Simpson's hold on the AFC rushing title; he had 1,407 yards for a league-high 5.3-yard average, caught 38 passes, and scored 12 touchdowns. Two years later, Armstrong again passed the 1,000-yard mark (1,008) and caught 39 passes. He retired after the 1980 season because of a chronic neck injury. His career totals include 4,453 yards and 131 receptions.

The New York Giants obtained free agent **Doug Kotar** from Pittsburgh for free agent Leo Gasienca in 1974. What a deal! Kotar earned a starting position as a rookie and went on to play seven seasons. He twice led the Giants in rushing—in 1976 when he had a personal-high 731 yards, and in 1978 with 625 yards. He missed all of 1980, but returned in 1981 to move past Eddie Price as the number-four rusher in Giants history with 3,380 yards. Kotar, who retired in 1982, passed away in 1983 after a battle with cancer.

Mike Thomas wasn't big (5-11, 190), but he still served as the Redskins' heavy-duty ball carrier for four years (1975-78). Thomas had played at Oklahoma and Nevada-Las Vegas before he earned NFL rookie of the year honors in 1975. He rushed for 919 yards and caught 40 passes in his first season. The next year he did even better, gaining 1,101 yards and scoring nine times. Thomas finished his six-year career with two seasons in San Diego. His career totals included 4,196 yards, 192 receptions, and 30 touchdowns.

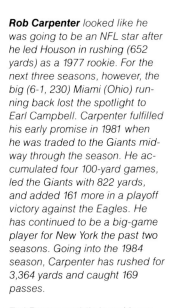

Rob Carpenter looked like he was going to be an NFL star after he led Houson in rushing (652 yards) as a 1977 rookie. For the next three seasons, however, the big (6-1, 230) Miami (Ohio) running back lost the spotlight to Earl Campbell. Carpenter fulfilled his early promise in 1981 when he was traded to the Giants mid-way through the season. He accumulated four 100-yard games, led the Giants with 822 yards, and added 161 more in a playoff victory against the Eagles. He has continued to be a big-game player for New York the past two seasons. Going into the 1984 season, Carpenter has rushed for 3,364 yards and caught 169 passes.

Ted Brown rapidly is making a shambles of the Minnesota record book. In 1983, the versatile five-year veteran from North Carolina State raised his career totals to 3,517 rushing yards, 248 receptions, and 33 touchdowns. Brown was the Vikings' top draft choice in 1979 and has led the club in rushing three times and receiving twice. His best year was 1981, when he ran for 1,063 yards (joining Chuck Foreman as the only Minnesota player with more than 1,000 yards) and caught 83 passes, third most that season in the NFL.

Roosevelt Leaks never has been able to recapture the magic he had before a knee injury slowed him down his senior year at Texas. Leaks was a consensus All-America as a junior (1973), but severely injured the knee in spring training prior to the 1974 season. As a senior, he had to take a back seat to freshman Earl Campbell. In the pros, he has played alongside some other outstanding backs—Lydell Mitchell in Baltimore and Joe Cribbs in Buffalo. Leaks has proven to be a devastating blocker and is almost unstoppable on short-yardage situations, especially at the goal line. In his nine years he has run for 2,406 yards and 28 touchdowns.

>

Ottis Anderson has been a record-breaker throughout his career. He shattered Chuck Foreman's season and career rushing standards at the University of Miami. Then Anderson (6-2, 222) went on to bigger things as a pro. The first draft choice of St. Louis in 1979, Anderson broke Earl Campbell's NFL rookie rushing record with 1,605 yards and set six club marks. In 1981, Anderson had his third consecutive 1,000-yard season (1,376) and passed up Jim Otis as the Cardinals' all-time leading rusher. Entering the 1984 season, he has rushed for 1,000 yards four times and has career totals of 6,190 rushing yards, 196 receptions, and 37 touchdowns.

Tony Collins had neither the size (5-11, 203) nor the reputation (coming from East Carolina) to create any great expectations for his NFL career. In only three years, however, Collins has become one of the most productive backs in pro football. As a rookie (1981), Collins led the Patriots in rushing (873 yards). He again led the team, and finished seventh in the NFL, with 632 yards in the strike-shortened 1982 season. In 1983, Collins became only the third New England player (Jim Nance and Sam Cunningham preceded him) to rush for 1,000 yards in a season. He gained 1,049 on a brilliant 4.8-yard average and scored 10 touchdowns. Collins had the best rushing game in the AFC in 1983 with 212 yards against the New York Jets.

When **Curtis Dickey** was chosen in the first round of the 1980 draft by Baltimore, he immediately was rated the fastest player in the NFL. In his career at Texas A&M, Dickey had won three NCAA 60-yard dash titles (including one in an NCAA-record 6.12 seconds). On the football field he gained 3,703 yards for the Aggies. In four years with the Colts, Dickey has used his speed and good size (6-0, 209) to continue piling up the yardage. He has led the Colts in rushing three times on the way to becoming the club's number-five career rusher (2,933 yards). In 1980, his 800 yards was the second most ever by a Colts' rookie, trailing only Alan Ameche's 961 yards in 1955. And in 1983 he became the second player in club history (after Lydell Mitchell) to gain 1,000 yards in a season (1,122).

THE SECOND DIMENSION

When **Tobin Rote** joined Green Bay in 1950, the Packers received two players in one—a quarterback and a halfback. Although the Rice star never lined up at halfback, he always ran like one. In his second season, Rote set the NFL record for yards rushing by a quarterback (523 for a league-leading 6.9-yard average). In his last year in Green Bay (1956), he not only threw the most touchdown passes in the NFL (18), he also scored 11 times. In 1957, Rote went to Detroit, and helped lead the Lions to the championship. After 10 years in the NFL, Rote played three years in Canada and three years with San Diego and Denver of the AFL. He finished his career with 3,128 rushing yards and 37 touchdowns.

When NFL scouts look for a potential star quarterback from the college ranks, running ability is not the first quality that comes to mind. The NFL quarterback must have arm strength, size, intelligence, accuracy, touch, anticipation, timing, judgment, leadership, poise, and, hopefully, mobility to avoid the rush. Mobility is a bonus, not a necessity; it often is translated as scrambling, not running. No right-thinking coach sends his quarterback out to run the ball often in the NFL.

Yet the NFL is full of quarterbacks who have run successfully, whether their excursions are planned or not. It isn't because the NFL goes after the great college running quarterbacks. As time has gone by, and one running quarterback after another has failed—remember Terry Baker, Gary Beban, Rex Kern, and Jack Mildren?—NFL teams have stopped drafting them for the quarterback position. Dan Reeves, Andy Johnson, Freddie Solomon, John Sciarra, and Nolan Cromwell (all of whom played quarterback in college) moved successfully into the NFL, but not at quarterback.

Most of the NFL's great running quarterbacks weren't outstanding college runners. Good college runners (or scramblers), yes, but their main appeal to NFL teams was as passers. That is true whether the NFL was in an era featuring many quarterbacks who were mobile (such as the 1980s), or in one having fewer quarterbacks who were threats to run if their receivers were covered (such as in the 1960s).

Regardless of when they played, running NFL quarterbacks have put more pressure on opposing defenses than predominantly pocket passers. Joe Theismann of Washington is tougher on defenses than the Rams' Vince Ferragamo because he sprints out, rolls out, scrambles, and runs. The defenders play a guessing game with Theismann, who has a multiplicity of options every time he takes a snap.

The most mobile and active quarterbacks in NFL history have used their talents different ways. Bobby Douglass preferred to run first and throw passes second. Roger Staubach would move around until he saw either an open receiver or a running lane for himself. Fran Tarkenton seemed to prefer to run around for the fun of it. He gained a lot of yards, but many of them came after long scrambles that tired out both the defenders and his receivers (open or not). Roman Gabriel preferred to run on third-and-short; he was like a fullback going straight at the defense. And Archie Manning, who had perhaps the best combination of running and passing ability in NFL history, ran out of sheer necessity.

Given the differing abilities of their offensive teammates and their own different mentalities, the best running quarterbacks, therefore, weren't necessarily the quarterbacks with the most yards. But they all used their special capacity to run to move the ball. It helped them accomplish what they were paid to do—win.

Fran Tarkenton scrambled for 18 years with the Vikings and Giants, eluding would-be tacklers before finally throwing a pass or taking off downfield. Tarkenton always was a threat, especially early in his career, when he ran for more than 300 yards in seven of eight seasons. Although he is best known for his passing records, Tarkenton gained 3,674 yards and scored 32 touchdowns on the ground.

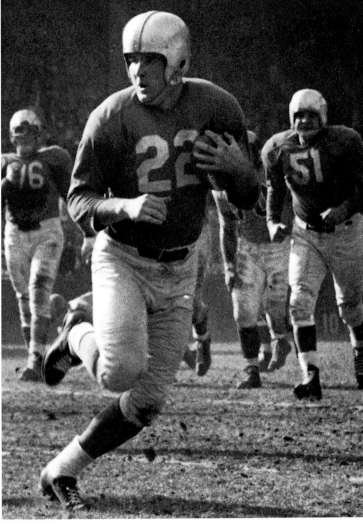

Otto Graham never rolled up the yardage on the ground that some quarterbacks did, but he always was a threat to run, especially near the goal line. Graham scored 33 career touchdowns, an average of better than one every 10 carries. A Single Wing tailback at Northwestern, Graham converted to the T formation with the Browns and led them to 10 championship games in his 10 seasons. His last two champion-ship games were perhaps his best games ever. In 1954 (a 56-10 victory over Detroit), he ran for three touchdowns and passed for three more. The next year, when the Browns defeated the Rams 38-14, he ran for two scores and passed for two. Graham had the aerial game to go with his running; counting his years in the AAFC, he is the number-two-rated passer in pro football history.

Bobby Layne would do anything to win. If it meant passing, he would pass; if it meant running, he would run. Layne was an All-America quarterback and pitcher at Texas who brought his hard-playing, hard-living show to the NFL. In his 15 pro seasons he helped lead Detroit to three NFL championships and, later, gain Pittsburgh respectability. He ran for 2,451 yards and 25 touch-downs in his career. His best year was 1952, when he ran for 411 yards in the regular season and scored the first touchdown in Detroit's 17-7 NFL Championship Game victory against Cleveland on a two-yard run.

Greg Landry made a big impression on the NFL in his first pro game—the 1968 Chicago College All-Star Game. The small-college All-America from Massachusetts continued his brilliant play—and especially his running—for 14 seasons with the Detroit Lions and Baltimore Colts. In his first season as a regular starter (1970), Landry ran for 350 yards and a 10.0-yard average. The next season he broke Tobin Rote's NFL rushing record for quarterbacks with 530 yards. His passing didn't suffer; he finished second in the NFC. He came close to breaking his own rushing record in 1972 with 524 yards. Injuries slowed Landry in his later years, but he still finished with a career rushing total of 2,654 yards and a 6.2-yard average.

V

>

At Mississippi, **Archie Manning** was perhaps the best combination running-passing quarterback in college football history. He threw 31 touchdown passes and ran for 25 more scores. He has demonstrated those same talents for 12 years in the NFL, although much of that time he spent in the New Orleans backfield trying to avoid being sacked. Manning has passed for 23,366 yards in his career, and has added 2,143 rushing yards (a 5.8-yard average).

<

Bobby Douglass was one college running quarterback who didn't change positions in the NFL. Perhaps the Kansas All-America should have—with his power and size (6-4, 225) he would have been an outstanding running back. Douglass averaged well over seven yards per carry in his first three years with Chicago. But in 1972, he really broke loose, shattering Greg Landry's record with 968 rushing yards. His 6.9-yard average is still the second best in NFL history for a minimum 100 carries. Douglass added 525 yards in 1973, but his passing wasn't efficient enough to allow him to maintain a starting position. He ended his career as a Green Bay reserve in 1978, having rushed for 2,654 yards and a 6.5-yard average.

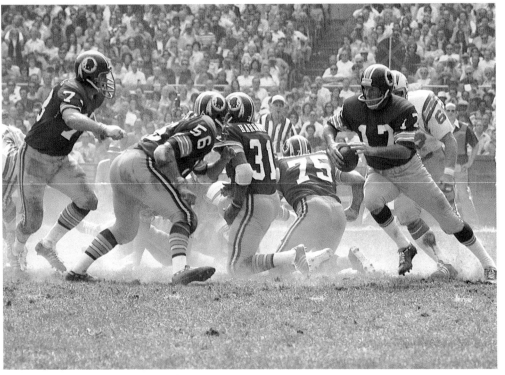

In 1961, **Billy Kilmer** must have looked like the perfect quarterback for 49ers head coach Red Hickey's new Shotgun formation. Kilmer, who had rushed for 803 yards, had led the nation in total offense as a Single Wing tailback at UCLA. So Hickey put him in his new backfield as a quarterback and let him run. Kilmer ran for 987 yards, a 5.2-yard average, and 15 touchdowns his first two seasons. He missed all of 1963 after being involved in an automobile accident and never was a great runner again. He played 14 more years in the NFL, including 4 years in New Orleans and 8 in Washington. He finished his career with 1,509 yards rushing and a 4.2-yard average.

When **Roger Staubach** was at the United States Naval Academy winning the Heisman Trophy, he loved to run. And when he joined the Dallas Cowboys in 1969, he continued his practice of dropping back, looking, and taking off; he averaged almost eight yards per carry in his first three years.

But in 1972, Staubach was injured on a run in a preseason game against the Rams and missed virtually the entire season. He became a more controlled scrambler after that, but still was inordinately successful. In his 11-year career, he ran for 2,264 yards and a 5.5-yard average.

It took several years in the NFL for **Terry Bradshaw** to learn how to find his secondary receiver and not simply to pull the ball down and go off to the races. When Bradshaw began limiting his running, the Steelers started winning Super Bowls. In the early stages of his career, however, defensing Bradshaw often could be like cov-

ering a fullback. The big (6-3, 210) Louisiana Tech quarterback would just run over defenders, a la Roman Gabriel. Bradshaw gained more than 200 yards in six of his first seven seasons. He had 2,252 career rushing yards and 32 touchdowns. He also rushed for 288 yards in playoff games.

 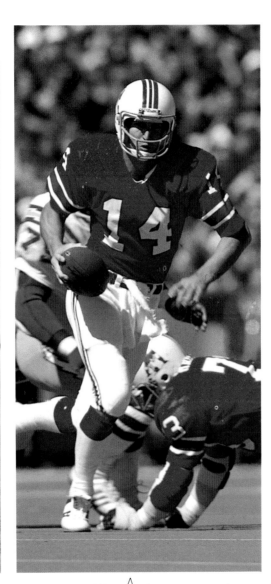 

Jim Zorn's value to Seattle is reflected in that he is not only the Seahawks' leading career passer, but their number-two rusher with 1,494 yards and 17 touchdowns. Zorn rushed for 1,164 yards and was a small-college All-America during a two-year career at Cal Poly-Pomona. In his first season with Seattle (1976) he broke Dennis Shaw's NFL rookie passing record with 2,571 yards. The former free agent has averaged five yards per carry in his career.

Before knee injuries slowed him down, **Steve Grogan** was the NFL's most mobile quarterback—also one of the most feared. Grogan initially gained a reputation in his second year with New England, when he ran for 397 yards and 12 touchdowns. Two years later, he had one of the best run-

ning seasons ever by a quarterback: 539 yards, a 6.7-yard average, and five touchdowns. Although he has run considerably less since 1980, when he had to miss part of the season resting his knees, Grogan still has career totals of 2,049 yards and 27 touchdowns.

Washington Redskins fans knew > their team had a mobile quarterback when **Joe Theismann** spent his first several years in the NFL returning punts. Theismann had been an All-America at Notre Dame, where he ran for more than 1,000 yards. He played three years in Canada and again had more than 1,000 yards and a six-yard average. Theismann has now played 10 seasons in the NFL, over the course of which he has run for 1,386 yards. His scrambling ability has allowed him to be one of the least sacked quarterbacks in the NFL.

Ken Anderson is usually thought of as one of the NFL's all-time efficient passers—a man who has led the league in passing four times and has thrown for 30,396 career yards. But he also is one of the best running quarterbacks in the league, a surprise considering he has played 13 years. Anderson has run for 2,033 yards in his career. One of his best rushing seasons came in 1981. That year he gained 320 yards, the best among NFL quarterbacks, and led the Bengals to Super Bowl XVI.

David Woodley might be the > NFL's most mobile active quarterback. Don Shula and the Miami Dolphins drafted Woodley in the eighth round in 1980, even though he had shared the quarterback position his entire career at LSU. There, he had scored 14 rushing touchdowns, but had thrown for only eight. Woodley has proven he can both pass and run in the NFL. After four years with the Dolphins (he now is with Pittsburgh), he had passed for 5,928 yards and 34 touchdowns and had rushed for 771 yards and nine touchdowns.

The Top 25 Rushers in NFL History

Name	Years	Att.	Yards	Avg.	TD
Jim Brown	1957-1965	2,359	12,312	5.2	106
Franco Harris	1972-1983*	2,881	11,950	4.1	91
Walter Payton	1975-1983*	2,666	11,625	4.4	78
O.J. Simpson	1969-1979	2,404	11,236	4.7	61
John Riggins	1971-79, 1981-83*	2,413	9,436	3.9	82
Jim Taylor	1958-1967	1,941	8,597	4.4	83
Joe Perry	1950-1963	1,737	8,378	4.8	53
Tony Dorsett	1977-1983*	1,834	8,336	4.5	53
Earl Campbell	1978-1983*	1,883	8,296	4.4	69
Larry Csonka	1968-74, 1976-79	1,891	8,081	4.3	64
Leroy Kelly	1964-1973	1,727	7,274	4.2	74
John Henry Johnson	1954-1966	1,571	6,803	4.3	48
Chuck Muncie	1976-1983*	1,547	6,651	4.3	71
Mark van Eeghen	1974-1983	1,652	6,650	4.0	37
Lawrence McCutcheon	1973-1981	1,521	6,578	4.3	26
Lydell Mitchell	1972-1980	1,675	6.534	3.9	30
Floyd Little	1967-1975	1,641	6,323	3.9	43
Don Perkins	1960-1968	1,500	6,217	4.1	42
Ottis Anderson	1979-1983*	1,401	6,190	4.4	34
Ken Willard	1965-1974	1,622	6,105	3.8	45
Calvin Hill	1969-74, 1976-81	1,452	6,083	4.2	42
Mike Pruitt	1976-1983*	1,430	6,034	4.2	41
Chuck Foreman	1973-1980	1,556	5,950	3.8	53
Larry Brown	1969-1976	1,530	5,875	3.8	35
Steve Van Buren	1944-1951	1,320	5,860	4.4	69

Leading Career Rushers by Team

Name	Years	Att.	Yards	Avg.	TD
Atlanta					
William Andrews	1979-1983*	1,253	5,772	4.6	29
Dave Hampton	1972-1976	885	3,490	3.9	17
Haskel Stanback	1974-1979	728	2,662	3.7	25
Jim Butler	1968-1971	609	2,250	3.7	7
Buffalo					
O.J. Simpson	1969-1977	2,123	10,183	4.8	57
Joe Cribbs	1980-1983	960	4,046	4.2	20
Wray Carlton	1960-1967	819	3,368	4.1	29
Cookie Gilchrist	1962-1964	676	3,058	4.5	31
Chicago					
Walter Payton	1975-1983*	2,666	11,625	4.4	78
Rick Casares	1955-1964	1,386	5,675	4.1	49
Gale Sayers	1965-1971	991	4,956	5.0	39
Roland Harper	1975-78, 1980-82	757	3,044	4.0	15
Cincinnati					
Pete Johnson	1977-1983*†	1,402	5,421	3.9	64
Essex Johnson	1968-1975	675	3,070	4.5	18
Boobie Clark	1973-1978	779	2,978	3.8	25
Paul Robinson	1968-1972	617	2,441	4.0	19
Cleveland					
Jim Brown	1957-1965	2,359	12,312	5.2	106
Leroy Kelly	1964-1973	1,727	7,247	4.2	74
Mike Pruitt	1976-1983*	1,430	6,034	4.2	41
Greg Pruitt	1973-1981	1,158	5,496	4.7	25
Dallas					
Tony Dorsett	1977-1983*	1,834	8,336	4.5	53
Don Perkins	1961-1968	1,500	6,217	4.1	42
Calvin Hill	1969-1974	1,166	5,009	4.3	39
Robert Newhouse	1972-1983	1,160	4,784	4.1	31
Denver					
Floyd Little	1967-1975	1,641	6,323	3.9	43
Otis Armstrong	1973-1980	1,023	4,453	4.4	25
Jon Keyworth	1973-1980	699	2,653	3.8	22
Dave Preston	1978-1983	479	1,793	3.7	10
Detroit					
Dexter Bussey	1974-1983*	1,171	5,014	4.3	18
Billy Sims	1980-1983*	1,001	4,419	4.4	37
Altie Taylor	1969-1976	1,165	4,297	3.7	24
Nick Pietrosante	1959-1965	938	3,933	4.2	28
Green Bay					
Jim Taylor	1958-1965	1,811	8,207	4.5	83
John Brockington	1971-1977	1,293	5,024	3.9	29
Tony Canadeo	1941-44, 1946-52	1,025	4,197	4.1	26
Clarke Hinkle	1932-1941	1,171	3,860	3.3	35
Houston					
Earl Campbell	1978-1983*	1,883	8,296	4.4	69
Hoyle Granger	1966-1970	732	3,339	4.6	17
Charlie Tolar	1960-1966	907	3,277	3.6	20
Ronnie Coleman	1974-1981	700	2,769	4.0	16
Indianapolis					
Lydell Mitchell	1972-1977	1,391	5,487	3.9	27
Lenny Moore	1956-1967	1,069	5,174	4.8	63
Tom Matte	1961-1972	1,200	4,646	3.9	45
Alan Ameche	1955-1960	964	4,045	4.2	40
Kansas City					
Ed Podolak	1969-1977	1,158	4,451	3.8	34
Abner Haynes	1960-1964	792	3,837	4.8	40
Mike Garrett	1966-1970	736	3,246	4.4	24
Curtis McClinton	1962-1969	762	3,124	4.1	18

Name	Years	Att.	Yards	Avg.	TD
Los Angeles Raiders					
Mark van Eeghen	1974-1981	1,475	5,907	4.0	35
Clem Daniels	1961-1967	1,133	5,103	4.5	30
Marv Hubbard	1969-1976	916	4,399	4.8	22
Pete Banaszak	1966-1978	963	3,772	3.9	47
Los Angeles Rams					
Lawrence McCutcheon	1973-1979	1,435	6,186	4.3	23
Dick Bass	1960-1969	1,218	5,417	4.4	34
Dan Towler	1950-1955	672	3,493	5.2	44
Les Josephson	1964-67, 1969-74	797	3,407	4.3	17
Miami					
Larry Csonka	1968-74, 1979	1,506	6,737	4.5	53
Mercury Morris	1969-1975	754	3,877	5.1	29
Jim Kiick	1968-1974	997	3,644	3.7	28
Delvin Williams	1978-1980	643	2,632	4.1	13
Minnesota					
Chuck Foreman	1973-1979	1,533	5,887	3.8	52
Bill Brown	1962-1974	1,786	5,757	3.2	52
Dave Osborn	1965-1975	1,173	4,320	3.7	29
Ted Brown	1979-1983*	863	3,517	4.1	26
New England					
Sam Cunningham	1973-79, 1981-82	1,385	5,453	3.9	43
Jim Nance	1965-1971	1,323	5,323	4.0	45
Don Calhoun	1975-1981	820	3,391	4.1	23
Larry Garron	1960-1968	763	2,981	3.9	14
New Orleans					
Chuck Muncie	1976-1980	787	3,386	4.3	28
George Rogers	1981-1983*	756	3,353	4.4	21
Tony Galbreath	1976-1980	760	2,865	3.8	27
Archie Manning	1971-1982	358	2,058	5.7	18
New York Giants					
Alex Webster	1955-1964	1,196	4,638	3.9	39
Ron Johnson	1970-1975	1,066	3,836	3.6	33
Frank Gifford	1952-60, 1962-64	840	3,609	4.3	34
Doug Kotar	1974-1981	900	3,380	3.8	20
New York Jets					
Emerson Boozer	1966-1975	1,291	5,104	4.0	52
Matt Snell	1964-1972	1,057	4,258	4.1	29
John Riggins	1971-1975	928	3,880	4.2	25
Bill Mathis	1960-1969	1,044	3,589	3.4	37
Philadelphia					
Steve Van Buren	1944-1951	1,320	5,860	4.4	69
Wilbert Montgomery	1977-1983*	1,264	5,749	4.5	43
Timmy Brown	1960-1967	850	3,703	4.4	29
Tom Woodeshick	1963-1971	831	3,563	4.3	21
Pittsburgh					
Franco Harris	1972-1983	2,881	11,950	4.1	91
John Henry Johnson	1960-1965	1,025	4,383	4.3	26
Dick Hoak	1961-1970	1,132	3,965	3.5	25
Rocky Bleier	1968, 1970-80	928	3,865	4.2	23
St. Louis					
Ottis Anderson	1979-1983*	1,401	6,190	4.4	34
Jim Otis	1973-1978	1,011	3,863	3.8	19
Johnny Roland	1966-1972	962	3,608	3.8	27
Charley Trippi	1947-1955	687	3,511	5.1	24
San Diego					
Paul Lowe	1960-1967	1,014	4,963	4.9	39
Chuck Muncie	1980-1983	759	3,258	4.3	43
Don Woods	1974-1980	713	2,858	4.0	16
Keith Lincoln	1960-1966	573	2,698	4.7	17

Name	Years	Att.	Yards	Avg.	TD
San Francisco					
Joe Perry	1950-60, 1963	1,475	7,344	4.9	50
Ken Willard	1965-1973	1,582	5,930	3.7	45
J.D. Smith	1956-1964	1,007	4,370	4.3	37
Hugh McElhenny	1952-1960	877	4,288	4.9	35
Seattle					
Sherman Smith	1976-1982	810	3,429	4.2	28
Jim Zorn	1976-1983*	301	1,494	5.0	17
Curt Warner	1983*	335	1,449	4.3	13
Dan Doornink	1979-1983*	402	1,315	3.3	11
Tampa Bay					
Ricky Bell	1977-1981	820	3,057	3.7	16
Jerry Eckwood	1979-1981	509	1,830	3.6	6
James Wilder	1981-1983*	351	1,334	3.8	11
Louis Carter	1976-1978	311	913	2.9	4
Washington					
Larry Brown	1969-1976	1,530	5,875	3.8	35
John Riggins	1976-79, 1981-83*	1,485	5,556	3.7	57
Mike Thomas	1975-1978	877	3,360	3.8	15
Don Bosseler	1957-1964	780	3,112	4.0	22

Still active going into 1984 season.   †Traded to San Diego prior to 1984 season.

Sherman Smith

Acknowledgements

Running Wild was a truly a labor of love for two life-long football fans. David Boss, the Vice President-Creative Director for NFL Properties and the man who initially conceptualized the project, was responsible for all photo selection. The pictures were chosen from the NFL Properties photo library. Beau Riffenburgh, also of NFL Properties, provided the book's editorial content.

However, a project such as *Running Wild* could not truly be the work of only two people. Bill Barron, Chuck Garrity, Jr., Jack Hand, and Jim Natal all served as editors and fact checkers. Andrew Apodaca was the proofreader. Ellen Galloway coordinated the flow of the copy.

Steven Escalante designed *Running Wild*. Jere Wright served as the coordinator with the typesetter, which was CAPCO of Los Angeles. Jim Chaffin and Miguel Elliott handled dark-room services for the designer. Charles Prince assisted in the mechanical reproduction of copy and photos.

Tina Thompson handled the overall production coordination with the printer.

All color processing work was prepared by Dai Nippon of Tokyo, Japan. Dai Nippon also printed the book.

Beau Riffenburgh
David Boss

A Photographic Note

The photographs displayed in *Running Wild* span 37 seasons of professional football. Within that period, the technology of cameras, lenses, and film improved dramatically, as is readily apparent in the quality of the photographs.

Many of the early photos were made with 4″ × 5″ format cameras, such as the bulky Graphex or Speed Graphix that featured 15- and 16-inch lenses and produced exact detail with extraordinary depth of field. Their problem was limited exposures; the negative carriers were cumbersome, and few photographs could be taken during a single game.

In the 1950s, the 35 millimeter camera—especially the single-lens reflex, to which a motor drive later was added—revolutionized game coverage; photographers were able to cover the action in depth. The evolution of telephoto lenses made these small cameras indispensible in covering the high-speed action of pro football.

The film makers kept pace. Over the years, Kodak's ever-expanding technology has provided fast-emulsion films that allowed full-color images, even in domed stadiums or at night games. Today, photographers choose from a wide range of films with varying emulsion speeds—everything from the popular Kodachrome 64 film to the new Kodacolor VR 1000 color print film.

The photographers, without whom this book would not have been possible, also have been practicing their individual styles and techniques for decades, documenting the development of pro football. A few, such as Vernon Biever (Packers), Nate Fine (Redskins), and Frank Rippon (49ers) have been covering their teams since the 1940s. Others, such as Malcolm Emmons, Dick Raphael, Russ Reed, Manny Rubio, Bob Smith, Tony Tomsic, Herb Weitman, and Lou Witt, have worked every Sunday of every season since the 1950s or 1960s. To these men, we especially express our gratitude, as well as to the younger photographers, who are building from their predecessors' firm base a standard of sports photography that is exceptional to behold.

Photography Credits

The Allens 69b, 81, 84a, 145b
Arthur Anderson 52a
Charles Aqua Viva 100a, 101b
John Biever 14-15, 70, 97, 106
Vernon Biever 46, 47a, 50, 77b, 90b, 94ab, 104, 135a
David Boss 61b, 62ab, 67a, 91, 117, 126-127b
Clifton Boutelle 90a, 134b
Chance Brockway 120b
Rob Brown 86
Buffalo Bills 45b
Chicago Bears 114
Melchior DiGiacomo 12-13
Patrick Downs 73
Malcolm Emmons 11, 30, 64a, 80b, 102a, 105ab, 110, 112, 121, 130a, 144b, 151, 152b
Nate Fine 27, 78a, 128a, 144a, 152c
James F. Flores 66, 80a, 92, 102-103, 118a, 129, 130b, 139b, 141, 153
George Gellatly 42, 115a, 127c, 150c
George Gojkovich 14b, 55
Pete J. Groh 156
Rod Hanna 31a, 45a, 118b, 132a
Jocelyn Hinsen 68a, 69a
Fred Kaplan 10, 64b, 140a
Amos Love 22, 71, 109a
Richard Mackson 111
Tak Makita 142b
John McDonough 20-21, 83
Al Messerschmidt Cover, 7, 16-17, 17b, 85, 157b
Peter Read Miller 18, 54b, 82b, 108
Bill Mount 72, 109b, Back Cover
Anthony Neste 120a
Darryl Norenberg 24, 32, 36, 49b, 52b, 63a, 65, 107a, 116b, 132-133, 135b, 155a
Jack O'Grady 136-137, 152a
Dick Raphael 47b, 49a, 53, 67b, 79, 115b, 138a, 139a, 146a
Russ Reed 134a
Frank Rippon 28ab, 29, 31b, 33b, 37a, 38, 41, 43, 56, 60. 123, 126a, 148, 150a
George Rose 6, 18-19, 96a
Ron Ross 146b
Dan Rubin 34-35, 44, 125
Manny Rubio 63b, 96b, 133b, 143, 147, 155c, 157a
Russ Russell 48
Carl Skalak, Jr. 74, 154
Bill Smith 140b
Robert L. Smith 12, 31c, 159
Chuck Solomon 20
Jay Spencer 92-93
Sports Illustrated 59b, 61a, 98-99
R.H. Stagg 78b, 84b, 119, 120c, 142a
Vic Stein 26, 59a, 116a, 124, 126-127a
Tony Tomsic 8, 9, 51, 77a, 94c, 100-101, 107bc, 128b, 138b, 155b
Corky Trewin 87
Jim Turner 54a
Herb Weitman 68b, 88-89, 95a, 131a
Lou Witt 22-23, 33a, 37b, 145a
Michael Zagaris 95b, 131b
Jack Zehrt 2-3
Howard Zryb 82a